Horatio Alger

Adrift in the City

Oliver Conrad's Plucky Fight

Horatio Alger

Adrift in the City
Oliver Conrad's Plucky Fight

ISBN/EAN: 9783743423855

Manufactured in Europe, USA, Canada, Australia, Japa

Cover: Foto ©Andreas Hilbeck / pixelio.de

Manufactured and distributed by brebook publishing software (www.brebook.com)

Horatio Alger

Adrift in the City

ADRIFT IN THE CITY

OR

OLIVER CONRAD'S PLUCKY FIGHT

BY

HORATIO ALGER, Jr.

AUTHOR OF "RAGGED DICK" SERIES, "TATTERED TOM"
SERIES, "LUCK AND PLUCK" SERIES

THE JOHN C. WINSTON CO.
PHILADELPHIA
CHICAGO   TORONTO

CONTENTS.

ADRIFT IN THE CITY;

OR,

OLIVER CONRAD'S PLUCKY FIGHT,

CHAPTER I.

TWO YOUNG ENEMIES.

"OLIVER, bring me that ball!" said Roland Kenyon, in a tone of command.

The speaker, a boy of sixteen, stood on the lawn before a handsome country mansion. He had a bat in his hand, and had sent the ball far down the street. He was fashionably dressed, and evidently felt himself a personage of no small consequence.

The boy he addressed, Oliver Conrad, was his junior by a year—not so tall, but broader and more thick-set, with a frank, manly face, and an air of independence and self-reliance.

He was returning home from school, and carried two books in his hand.

Oliver was naturally obliging, but there was something he did not like in the other's imperious tone, and his pride was touched.

"Are you speaking to me?" he demanded quietly.

"Of course I am.   Is there any other Oliver about?"

"When you ask a favor, you had better be polite about it."

"Bother politeness!   Go after that ball! Do you hear?" exclaimed Roland angrily.

Oliver eyed him calmly.

"Go for it yourself," he retorted.   "I don't intend to run on your errands."

"You don't?" exclaimed Roland furiously.

"Didn't I speak plainly enough?   I meant what I said."

"Go after that ball this instant!" shrieked Roland, stamping his foot; "or I'll make you!"

"Suppose you make me do it," said Oliver contemptuously, opening the gate, and entering the yard.

Roland had worked himself into a passion, and this made him reckless of consequences. He threw the bat in his hand at Oliver, and if the latter had not dodged quickly it would have seriously injured him. At the same time Roland rushed impetuously upon the boy who had offended him by his independence.

To say that Oliver kept calm under this aggravated attack would be incorrect. His eyes flashed with anger. He threw his books upon the lawn, and put himself in an instant on guard. A moment, and the two boys were engaged in a close struggle.

Roland was taller, and this gave him an advantage; but Oliver was the more sturdy and agile. He clasped Roland around the waist, lifted him off his feet, and laid him, after a brief resistance, on the lawn.

"You'd better not attack me again!" he said, looking with flushed face at his fallen foe.

Roland was furious. He sprang to his feet and flung himself upon Oliver, but with so little discretion that the latter, by a well-planted blow, immediately felled him to the ground, and, warned by the second attack, planted his knee on Roland's breast, thus preventing him from rising.

"Let me up!" shrieked Roland furiously, struggling desperately but ineffectually.

"Will you let me alone, then?"

"No, I won't!" returned Roland, who in his anger lost sight of prudence.

"Then you may lie there till you promise," said Oliver composedly.

"Get up, you bully!" screamed Roland.

"You are the bully. You attacked me, or I should never have touched you," said Oliver.

"I'll tell my father," said Roland.

"Tell, if you want to," said Oliver, his lip curling.

"He'll have you well beaten."

"I don't think he will."

"So you defy him, then?"

"No; I defy nobody. But I mean to defend myself from violence."

"What's the matter with you two boys? Oliver, what are you doing?"

The speaker was Mr. Kenyon's gardener, John Bradford, a sensible man and usually intelligent. Oliver often talked with him, and treated him respectfully, as he deserved. Roland was foolish enough to look down upon him because he was a poor man and occupied a subordinate position.

Oliver rose from the ground and let up his adversary.

"We have had a little difficulty, Mr. Bradford," he said. "Roland may tell you if he likes."

"What is the trouble, Roland?" enquired the gardener.

"None of your business!" answered Roland insolently.

"You are very polite," said the gardener.

"I don't feel called upon to be polite to my father's hired man," remarked Roland unpleasantly.

"If he won't answer your question, I will," said Oliver. "Roland commanded me to run and get his ball, and I didn't choose to do it. He attacked me, and I defended myself. That is all there is about it."

"No, it isn't all there is about it," said Roland passionately. "You have insulted me, and you are going to be flogged. You may just make up your mind to that."

"How have I insulted you?"

"You threw me down."

"Suppose I hadn't. What would have happened to me?"

"I would have whipped you if you hadn't taken me by surprise."

Oliver shrugged his shoulders.

Apparently Roland didn't propose to renew the fight. Oliver watched him warily, suspecting a sudden attack, but it was not made. Roland turned toward the house, merely discharging this last shaft at his young conqueror:

"You'll get it when my father gets home."

"Your ball is in the road," said the gardener. "It will be lost."

"No, it won't. Oliver will have to bring it in yet."

"I am afraid he means mischief, Oliver," said the gardener, turning to our hero as Roland slammed the front door upon entering.

"I suppose he does," said Oliver quietly.

"It isn't the first attempt he has made to order me around."

"He is a very disagreeable boy," said Bradford.

"He is the most disagreeable boy I know," said Oliver. "I can get along with any of the other boys, except Jim Cameron, his chosen friend. He's pretty much the same sort of fellow as Roland—only, not being rich, he can't put on so many airs."

"You talk of Roland being rich," said the gardener. "He has no right to be called so."

"His father has property, I suppose?"

"Mr. Kenyon was poor enough when he married your mother. All the property he owns came from her."

"Is that true, Mr. Bradford?" asked Oliver thoughtfully.

"Yes; didn't you know it?"

"I have sometimes thought so."

"There is no doubt about it. It excited a good deal of talk—your mother's will."

"Did she leave all her property to Mr. Kenyon, John?"

"So he says, and he shows a will that has been admitted to probate."

Oliver was silent for a moment. Then he spoke:

"If my mother chose to leave all to him, I have not a word to say. She had a right to do as she pleased."

"But it seems singular. She loved you as much as any mother loves her son ; yet she disinherited you."

"I will not complain of anything she did, Mr. Bradford," said Oliver soberly.

"Suppose she didn't do it, Master Oliver ?"

"What do you mean, Mr. Bradford ?" asked the boy, fixing his eyes upon the gardener's face.

"I mean that there are some in the village who think there has been foul play—that the will is not genuine."

"Do you think so, Mr. Bradford ?"

"Knowing your mother, and her love for you, I believe there's been some fraud practised, and that Mr. Kenyon is at the bottom of it."

"I wish I knew," said Oliver. "It isn't

the money I care about so much, but I don't like to think that my mother preferred Mr. Kenyon to me."

"Wait patiently, Oliver; it'll all come out some day."

Just then Roland appeared at the front door and called out, in a tone of triumphant malice:

"Come right in, Oliver; my father wants to see you."

Oliver and the gardener exchanged glances. Then the boy answered:

"You may tell your father I am coming," and walked quietly toward the front door.

"I've told him all about it," said Roland.

"Are you sure you have told your father all?"

"Yes, I have."

"That's all I want. If you have told him all, he must see that I am not to blame."

"You'll find out. He's mad enough."

Oliver knew enough of his step-father to accept this as probable.

"Now, for it," he thought, and followed Roland into his father's presence.

CHAPTER II.

BENJAMIN KENYON, the father of Roland and Oliver's step-father, was a man of fifty or more. He had a high narrow forehead, small eyes, and a scanty supply of coarse black hair rimming a bald crown with a fringe in the shape of a horse-shoe. His expression was crafty and insincere. A tolerable judge of physiognomy would at once pronounce him as a man not to be trusted.

He turned upon Oliver with a frown, and said harshly:

"How dared you assault my son Rola?

"It was he who assaulted me, Mr. ——yon," answered Oliver quietly.

"Do you deny that you felled him to the earth twice?"

"I threw him over twice, if that is what you mean, sir."

"If that is what I mean! Don't be impertinent, sir."

"I have not been—thus far."

"Do you think I shall allow you to make a brutal assault upon my son, you young reprobate?"

"If you call me by that name again I shall refuse to answer you," said Oliver with spirit.

"Do you hear that, father?" interrupted Roland, anxious to prejudice his father against his young enemy.

"I hear it," said Mr. Kenyon; "and you may rely upon it that I shall take notice of it, too. So you have no defence to make, then?"

This last question was, of course, addressed to Oliver.

"I will merely state what happened, Mr. Kenyon. Roland had batted his ball far out on the road. He ordered me to go for it, and I refused."

"You refused?"

"Yes, sir."

"And why?"

"Because I am not subject to your son's orders."

"It is because you are selfish and disobliging."

"No, sir. If Roland had asked me, as a favor, to get the ball, I would have done it, being nearer to it than he, but I did not choose to obey his orders."

"He has a right to order you about," said Mr. Kenyon, frowning.

"I don't admit it," said Oliver.

"Is he not older than you?"

"Yes, sir."

"Then you must obey him?"

"I am sorry to differ with you, Mr. Kenyon, but I cannot see it in that light."

"It makes very little difference in what light you see it," sneered Mr. Kenyon. "I command you to obey him!"

Roland listened with triumphant malice, and nodded his head with satisfaction.

"Do you hear that?" he said insolently.

Oliver eyed him calmly.

"Yes, I hear it," he said.

"Then you'd better remember it next time."

" Where is the ball now ? " asked Mr. Kenyon.

" In the street."

" Oliver, you may go and get it, and bring it to Roland."

Roland laughed—a little low, chuckling laugh that was very exasperating to Oliver. Our hero's naturally pleasant face assumed a firm and determined expression. He was about to make a declaration of independence.

"Do you ask me to go for this ball as a favor ? " he asked, turning to his step-father.

" No," returned the latter harshly. " I command you to do it without question, and at once."

" Then, sir, much as I regret it, I must refuse to obey you."

Oliver was pale but firm.

Mr. Kenyon's face, on the contrary, was flushed and angry."

" Do you defy me ? " he roared furiously.

" I defy no one, sir, but you require me to do what would put me in the power of your son. If I consented, there would be no end to his attempts to tyrannize over me."

"Are you aware that I am your natural guardian, sir—that the law delegates to me supreme authority over you, you young reprobate?" demanded Mr. Kenyon, working himself into an ungovernable passion.

Oliver did not reply.

"Speak, I order you!" exclaimed his step-father, stamping his foot.

"I did not speak sooner because you called me a young reprobate, sir. I answer now that I will sooner leave your house and go out into the world to shift for myself than allow Roland to trample upon me and order me about like a dog."

"Enough of this! Roland, go downstairs and get my cane."

"I'll go," said Roland, with alacrity.

It was a welcome commission. Smarting with a sense of his own recent humiliating defeat, nothing could be sweeter than to see his victorious adversary beaten in his own presence. Of course he understood that it was for this purpose his father wanted the cane.

There was silence in the room while Roland

was gone. Oliver was rapidly making up his mind what he would do.

Roland ran upstairs with the cane.

"Here it is, father," he said, extending it to Mr. Kenyon.

"I will give you one more chance, Oliver," said his step-father. "You have insulted my son and rebelled against my authority, but I do not want to proceed to violence unless I am absolutely obliged to. I command you once more to go and get Roland's ball."

"If you command me, sir, I must answer as I did before—I must refuse."

Roland looked relieved. He feared that Oliver would yield, and so escape the beating he was anxious to witness.

"Aint he impudent!" he ejaculated. "Are you going to stand that, father?"

"No, I am not," said Mr. Kenyon grimly. "I will make him repent bitterly his rebellious course. Come here, sir—or no," and a smile lighted up his face, "it is more befitting that your punishment should come from the one whom you have insulted. Roland, take the cane and give Oliver a dozen strokes with it."

"You'll back me up, won't you?" asked Roland cautiously.

"Yes, I will back you up. There is nothing to fear."

"I guess father and I'll be a match for him," thought the brave Roland.

He took the cane and advanced toward Oliver with it uplifted.

"If you touch me it will be at your peril!" said Oliver, pale but firm.

Roland looked at his father, and received a nod of encouragement.

He hesitated no longer, but, with a look of triumphant spite, lifted the cane and rushed toward Oliver. It did not fall where it was intended, for, with a spring, Oliver wrested it from his grasp and threw it out of the window. Then, without a word, leaving father and son gazing into each other's faces with mingled wrath and dismay, he left the room.

"Are you going to allow this, father?" asked Roland in a tone of disappointment. "Oliver doesn't pay you the least respect."

Mr. Kenyon was not a brave or a resolute man. He was a man capable of petty tyranny, but one to be cowed by manly opposition. It occurred to him that in seeking to break Oliver's spirit, he had undertaken a difficult task. So he hardly knew what to say.

"Shall I run after him?" asked Roland.

"No," said his father. "I will take a little time to consider what is to be done with him. I'll make him rue this day, you may depend upon it."

"I hope you will," said Roland. "I don't mind so much about myself," he added artfully, "but I hate to see him treat you so."

"I'll break his proud spirit," said Mr. Kenyon, biting his lip. "I'll find a way, you may depend upon it."

CHAPTER III.

THE YOUNG RIVALS.

WHEN Oliver left the house he was uncertain whither to bend his steps. The supper hour was near at hand, but it would hardly be pleasant under the circumstances to meet his step-father and Roland at the tea-table. He preferred to go without his evening meal.

As he walked slowly along the main street on which his step-father's house was situated, plunged in thought, he was called to himself by a slap on his shoulder.

"What are you thinking about, Oliver?" was asked, in a cheery voice.

"Frank Dudley!" said our hero, "you're just the boy I want to see."

"Do I owe you any money?" asked Frank, in mock alarm.

"Not that I know of."

"Then it's all right. I am glad to meet you, too. Where are you going?"

"I don't know."

"Have you had supper?"

"No."

"Then come home with me. You haven't taken supper at our house for a long time."

"So I will," responded Oliver with alacrity.

"I see how it is," said Frank. "They were going to send you to bed without your supper, and my invitation brings you unexpected relief."

"You are partly right. But for your invitation I should have had no supper."

"What is it all about, Oliver? What's the matter?"

"I'll tell you, Frank. Mr. Kenyon and I have had a quarrel."

"I am not surprised at that. I don't admire the man, even if he is your step-father."

"Oh, you needn't check your feelings on my account. I never could like him."

"How did the trouble begin?"

"It began with Roland. I'll tell you about it," and Oliver told what had occurred.

Frank listened in silence.

"I think you did right," he said. "I wouldn't submit to be ordered round by such a popinjay. He's the most disagreeable boy I know, and my sister thinks so, too."

"He seems to admire your sister."

"She doesn't appreciate his attentions. He's always coming up and wanting to walk with her, though she is cool enough with him."

Oliver was glad to hear this. To tell the truth, he had a boyish fancy for Carrie Dudley himself, which was not surprising, for she was the prettiest girl in the village. Though he had not supposed she looked favorably upon Roland, it was pleasant to be assured of this by the young lady's brother.

"Poor Roland!" he said, smiling. "Your sister may give him the heartache."

"Oh, I guess his heart's pretty tough. But here we are."

Frank Dudley's father was a successful physician. His mother was dead, and her place in the household was supplied by his father's sister, Miss Pauline Dudley, who, though an old maid, had a sunny temperament and kindly disposition. The doctor's house, though not as pretentious as Mr. Kenyon's, was unusually pleasant and attractive.

"Aunt Pauline," said Frank to his aunt, who was sitting on a rocking chair on the front piazza, "I have brought Oliver home to supper."

"I am very glad to see you, Oliver," said Miss Dudley. "I wish you would come oftener."

"Thank you, Miss Dudley; I am always glad to come here. It is so pleasant and social compared with——"

He paused, thinking it not in good taste to refer unfavorably to his own home.

"I understand," said Miss Dudley. "You must be lonely at home."

"I am," said Oliver briefly.

"Not much company, and that poor," whispered Frank.

Oliver nodded assent.

Here Carrie Dudley appeared and cordially welcomed Oliver.

"Carrie seems glad to see you, Oliver," said

Frank; "but you must not feel too much elated. It's only on account of your relation-ship to Roland. She's perfectly infatuated with that boy."

Like most brothers, Frank liked to tease his sister.

"Roland!" repeated Carrie, tossing her head. "I hope I have better taste than to like him."

"It's all put on, Oliver. You mustn't believe what she says."

"Didn't I see Roland walking with you yesterday?" asked Oliver, willing to join in the teasing.

"Because I couldn't get rid of him," retorted Carrie.

"He thinks you are over head and ears in love with him," said Frank.

"I don't believe he thinks anything of the kind. If he does, he is very much mistaken; that is all I can say."

"Don't tease your sister any more, Frank," said Oliver. "I don't believe she admires Roland any more than I do."

"Thank you, Oliver. I am glad to have

you on my side," said the young lady graciously. "I shouldn't mind if I never saw Roland Kenyon."

"Stop your quarrelling, young people, and walk in to supper," said Miss Pauline.

"Where is your father to-night, Frank?" asked Oliver, as they ranged themselves round the neat supper table.

"He has been sent for to Claremont. He won't be back till late, probably. You will please look upon me as the head of the household while he is away."

· "I will, most learned doctor."

The evening meal passed pleasantly. Oliver could not help contrasting it with the dull and formal supper he was accustomed to take at home, and his thoughts found utterance.

"I wish I had as pleasant a home as you, Frank."

"You had better come and live with us, Oliver."

"I should like to."

"Suppose you propose it to Mr. Kenyon. I don't believe he prizes your society very much."

"Nor I. He wouldn't mind being rid of me, but Roland would probably object to my coming here."

"I didn't think of that."

"I should like to have you with us, Oliver," said Miss Pauline. "You would be company for Frank, and could help keep him straight."

"As if I needed it, Aunt Pauline! All the same, I should enjoy having Oliver here, and so would Carrie."

"Yes, I should," said the young lady unhesitatingly.

Oliver was well pleased, and expressed his satisfaction.

After supper they adjourned to the parlor, and presently Carrie sat down to the piano and played and sang some popular songs, Frank and Oliver joining in the singing.

While they were thus engaged a ring was heard at the door-bell.

"That's Roland, I'll bet a hat," said Frank. "It's one of his courting evenings."

It proved to be Roland.

He entered with a stiff bow.

"Good-evening, Miss Carrie," he said, a little awkwardly.

"Good-evening, Mr. Kenyon," said the young lady distantly. "Will you be seated?"

"Thank you. Good-evening, Frank."

"Good-evening. May I introduce you to Mr. Oliver Conrad?"

"You here?" said Roland, surprised.

Being near-sighted, he had not before noticed our hero's presence.

"I am here," said Oliver briefly.

"We were singing as you entered, Roland," said Frank mischievously. "Won't you favor us with a melody?"

"I don't sing," said Roland stiffly.

"Indeed! Oliver is quite a singer."

"I was not aware he was so accomplished," said Roland, unable to suppress a sneer.

"I suppose he doesn't often sing to you."

"I shouldn't like to trouble him. I should be very glad to hear you sing, Miss Carrie."

"If Frank and Oliver will join in. I don't like to sing alone."

A song was selected, and the three sang

it through. Sitting at the other end of the room, Roland, who greatly admired Carrie, was tormented with jealousy as he saw Oliver at her side, winning smiles and attention which he had never been able to win. He could not help wishing that he, too, were able to sing. If Oliver had made himself ridiculous, it would have comforted him, but our hero had a strong and musical voice, and acquitted himself very creditably.

"It's a pity you don't sing, Roland," said Frank.

"I wouldn't try to sing unless I could sing well," said Roland.

"Is he hitting you or me, Oliver?" asked Frank.

"You sing well," said Roland.

"Then it's you, Oliver!"

Oliver smiled, but took no notice of the remark.

Roland rose to go a little after nine. He had not enjoyed the evening. It was very unsatisfactory to see the favor with which his enemy was regarded by Carrie Dudley. He had not the art to conceal his dislike of our hero.

"You'd better come home," he said, turning to Oliver. "Father objects to our being out late."

"I know when to come home," said Oliver briefly.

"You'd better ask leave before you go out to supper again."

"If you have no more to say I will bid you good-evening," said Oliver quietly.

"You see what a pleasant brother I have," said Oliver after Roland's departure.

"It's a good thing to have somebody to look after you," said Carrie. "I wish Frank had such a guardian and guide."

"I shall have, when Roland is my brother-in-law," retorted Frank.

"Then you'll have to go without one forever."

"Girls never say what they mean, Oliver."

"Sometimes they do."

Meanwhile Roland was trudging home in no very good humor.

"I'd give fifty dollars to see Oliver well thrashed," he muttered. "He is interfering with me in everything."

CHAPTER IV.

MR. KENYON'S SECRET.

WHILE this rivalry was going on between Oliver and Roland, Mr. Kenyon, remaining at home, had had a surprise and a disagreeable one.

At half-past seven Roland left the house. At quarter to eight the door-bell rang, and Mr. Kenyon was informed that a gentleman wished to see him.

He was looking over some business papers and the interruption did not please him.

"Who is it?" he demanded impatiently.

"A gentleman."

"So I suppose. What is his name?"

"He is a stranger, sir, and he didn't give me his name. He said he wanted to see you partic'lar."

"Well, you may bring him up," said Mr.

Kenyon, folding up his papers with an air of resignation.

He looked up impatiently as the visitor entered, and straightway a look of dismay overspread his countenance.

The visitor was a dark-complexioned man of about forty-five, with bushy black whiskers.

"Dr. Fox!" ejaculated Mr. Kenyon mechanically.

The visitor chuckled.

"So you know me, Mr.——ahem! Mr. Kenyon. I feared under the circumstances you might have forgotten me."

"How came you here?" demanded Kenyon abruptly.

"A little matter of business brought me to New York, and a matter of curiosity brought me to this place."

"How did you trace me to—to Brentville?" asked Mr. Kenyon, with evident uneasiness.

"I suppose that means you didn't wish to be traced, eh?"

"And suppose I did not?"

"I am really sorry to have disturbed you, Mr. Crandall—I beg pardon, Kenyon; but I thought you might like to hear directly from your wife.''

''For Heaven's sake, hush!'' exclaimed Kenyon, looking round him nervously.

He rose, and, walking to the door, shut it, first peering into the hall to see if anyone were listening.

Dr. Fox laughed again.

''It's well to be cautious,'' he said. ''I quite approve of it—under the circumstances, Mr. Kenyon,'' he proceeded, leering at him with unpleasant familiarity. ''You're a deep one! I give you credit for being deeper than I supposed. You've played your cards well, that's a fact.''

Mr. Kenyon bit his finger-nails to the quick in his alarm and irritation. He would like to have choked the man who sat before him, if he had dared, and possessed the requisite strength.

'' You only made one mistake, my dear sir. You shouldn't have tried to deceive me. You should have taken me into your confidence. You might have known I would find out your little game.''

"Dr. Fox," said Mr. Kenyon, frowning, "your tone is very offensive. You will bear in mind that you are addressing a gentleman."

"Ho! ho!" laughed the visitor. "I really beg pardon," he said, marking the dark look on the face of the other. "No offence is intended. In fact, I was rather expressing my admiration for your sharpness. It was an admirable plan, that of yours."

"I don't care for compliments. Why have you sought me out?"

"A moment's patience, Mr. Kenyon. I was about to say Crandall—force of habit, sir. As I remarked, it was a capital plan to commit your wife to an insane asylum, and then take possession of her property. Did you have any difficulty about that, by the way?"

"None of your business!" snapped Mr. Kenyon.

"I am naturally a little curious on the subject."

"Confound your curiosity!"

"And so—ho! ho!—you are popularly regarded as a widower? Perhaps you have reared a monument in the cemetery to the dear departed? Ho! ho!"

"This is too much, sir!" exploded Kenyon, in wrath. "Drop this subject, or I may do you a mischief."

"You'd better think twice before you permit your feelings to overmaster you," said the stranger significantly. "That's an ugly secret I possess of yours. What would the good people of Brentville say if they knew that your wife, supposed to be dead, is really confined in an insane asylum, while you, without any sanction of law, are living luxuriously on her wealth? I think, Mr. Kenyon, they would be very apt to lynch you."

"You have nothing to complain of, at least. You are well paid for the care of—of the person you mention."

"I am paid my regular price—that is all, sir."

"Is not that enough?"

"Under the circumstances, it is not."

"Why not?"

"Do you need to ask? To begin with, your wife——"

"Hush!" said Kenyon nervously. "Call her Mrs. Crandall."

"Mrs. Crandall, if you will. Well, Mrs. Crandall is as sane as you are."

"Then she is less trouble."

"Not at all! She is continually imploring us to release her. It is quite a strain upon our feelings, I do assure you."

"Your feelings!" repeated Kenyon disdainfully.

Dr. Fox laughed.

"Really," he said, "I am quite affected at times by her urgency."

"Does she—ever mention me?" asked Mr. Kenyon slowly.

"Yes, but it wouldn't flatter you to hear her. She speaks of you as a cruel tyrant, who has separated her from her boy. His name is Oliver, isn't it?"

"Yes."

"She mourns for him, and prays to see him once more before she dies."

"Is her physical health failing?" enquired Kenyon, with sudden hopefulness.

"No; that is the strangest part of it. She

8

retains her strength. Apparently she is determined to husband her strength, and resolved to live on in the hope of some day being restored to her son."

Mr. Kenyon gnawed his nails more viciously than before. It had been his cherished hope that the wife whom he had so cruelly consigned to a living death would succumb beneath the accumulated weight of woe, and relieve him of all future anxiety by dying in reality. The report just received showed that such hopes were fallacious.

"Well, sir," he commenced, after a brief pause. "I do not wish to prolong this interview. Tell me why you have tracked me here? What is it you require?"

"The fact is, Mr. Kenyon,—you'll excuse my dropping the name of Crandall,—I want some money."

"A month since I paid, through my agent, your last quarterly bill. No more money will be due you till the 1st of December."

"I want a thousand dollars," said the visitor quietly.

"What!" ejaculated Kenyon.

"I want a thousand dollars before I leave Brentville."

"You won't get it from me!"

"Consider a moment, Mr. Crandall,—I mean Mr. Kenyon,—the result of my publishing this secret of yours. I understand that your wife's property, which you wrongfully hold, amounts to a quarter of a million of dollars. If all were known, your step-son Oliver and his mother would step into it, and you would be left out in the cold. Disagreeable, very! Can't you introduce me to Oliver?"

Mr. Kenyon's face was a study. He was like a fly in the meshes of a spider, absolutely helpless.

"If I give you a check," he said, "will you leave Brentville at once?"

"First thing to-morrow morning."

"Can't you go before?"

"Not conveniently. The next town is five miles away, and I don't like night travel."

Mr. Kenyon opened his desk and hastily dashed off a check.

"Now," said he, "leave, and don't come back."

"You waive ceremony with a vengeance, Mr. Kenyon," said the visitor, depositing the check in his pocket-book with an air of satisfaction. "Permit me to thank you for your liberality."

As he was about to leave the room Roland dashed in. The two looked at each other curiously.

"Is this Oliver?" asked Dr. Fox.

"No, it is my son Roland. Good-evening."

"I am glad to make the young gentleman's acquaintance. Hope he'll inherit his father's virtues, ha, ha!"

"Who is that, father?" asked Roland when the visitor had retired.

"A mere acquaintance, Roland—a man with whom I have had a little business."

"I don't like him."

"Nor I. But I must bid you good-night, my son. I am tired and need rest."

"I wanted to speak to you about Oliver."

"We will defer that till morning."

"Good-night, then!" and Roland left his father a prey to anxieties which kept him awake for hours.

CHAPTER V.

MR. KENYON felt that a sword was impending over his head which might at any time fall and destroy him. Four years before he had married Mrs. Conrad, a wealthy widow, whose acquaintance he had made at a Saratoga boarding-house. Why Mrs. Conrad should have been willing to sacrifice her independence for such a man is one of the mysteries which I do not pretend to solve. I can only record the fact. Oliver was away at the time, or his influence—for he never fancied Mr. Kenyon—might have turned the scale against the marriage.

Mr. Kenyon professed to be wealthy, but his new wife never was able to learn in what his property consisted or where it was located. Shortly after marriage he tried to get the management of his wife's property into his

own hands ; but she was a cautious woman,—a
trait she inherited from Scotch ancestry,—and,
moreover, she was devotedly attached to her
son Oliver. She came to know Mr. Kenyon
better after she had assumed his name, and to
distrust him more. Three months had not
passed when she bitterly repented having
accepted him ; but she had taken a step which
she could not retrace. She allowed Mr. Kenyon a liberal sum for his personal expenses,
and gave a home to his son Roland, who was
allowed every advantage which her own son
enjoyed. Further than this she was not
willing to go, and Mr. Kenyon was, in
consequence, bitterly disappointed. He had
supposed his wife to be of a more yielding
temperament.

So matters went on for three years. Then
Mr. Kenyon all at once fancied himself in very
poor health, at any rate he so represented.
He induced a physician to recommend travelling, and to urge the importance of his wife
accompanying him. She fell into the trap,
for it proved to be a trap. The boys were left
at home, at a boarding-school, and Mr. and

Mrs. Kenyon set out on their travels. They sailed for Cuba, where they remained two months; then they embarked for Charleston. In the neighborhood of Charleston Mr. Kenyon was enabled at length to carry out his nefarious design. He made the acquaintance of Dr. Fox, an unprincipled keeper of a private insane asylum, and left Mrs. Kenyon in his charge, under the name of Mrs. Crandall, with the strictest orders that under no circumstances should she be permitted to leave the asylum.

Three months from the time of his departure he reappeared in Brentville, wearing deep mourning—a widower. According to his account, Mrs. Kenyon had been attacked by a malignant fever, and died in four days. He also produced a will, made by his wife, conveying to him absolutely her property, all and entire. The only reference to her son Oliver was couched in these terms:

"I commend my dear son Oliver to my husband's charge, fully satisfied that he will provide for him in all ways as I would myself, urging him to do all in his power to promote my dear Oliver's welfare, and prepare him for a creditable and useful position in the world."

But for this clause doubts would have been expressed as to the genuineness of the will. As it was, it was generally supposed to be authentic, but Mrs. Kenyon was severely criticised for reposing so much confidence in her husband, and leaving Oliver wholly dependent upon him.

It was a great blow to Oliver,—his mother's death,—and the world seemed very lonely to him. Besides, he could not fail to notice a great difference in the manner of Mr. Kenyon and Roland toward him. The former laid aside his velvety manner and assumed airs of command. He felt secure in the position he had so wrongfully assumed, and hated Oliver all the more because he knew how much he had wronged him.

Roland, too, was quick to understand the new state of things. He was older than Oliver, and tried to exact deference from him on that account. His father had promised to make him his chief heir, and both had a tacit understanding that Oliver was to be treated as a poor relation, with no money and no rights except such as they might be graciously pleased to accord.

But Oliver did not fit well into this rôle. He was too spirited and too independent to be browbeaten, and did not choose to flatter or fawn upon his step-father though he did bear the purse.

The outbreak recorded in the first chapter would have come sooner had Oliver been steadily at home. But he had spent some weeks in visiting a cousin out of town, and was thus saved from a conflict with Roland. Soon after he came home the scene already described took place.

Thus far things had gone to suit Mr. Kenyon. But the arrival of Dr. Fox, and his extortionate demand, with the absolute certainty that it would be followed at frequent intervals by others, was like a clap of thunder in a clear sky. Henceforth peril was imminent. At any time his wife might escape from her asylum, and appear on the scene to convict him of conspiracy and falsehood. This would mean ruin. At any time Dr. Fox, if his exactions were resisted, might reveal the whole plot, and this, again, would be destruction. If not, he might be emboldened, by the possession of a damaging secret, to the most exorbitant demands.

These thoughts worried Mr. Kenyon, and robbed him of sleep.

What should he, or could he do?

Two things seemed desirable—to get rid of Oliver, and to leave Brentville for some place where neither Dr. Fox nor his injured wife could seek him out.

The more he thought of this way out of the difficulty the better he liked it. There was nothing to bind him to Brentville except the possession of a handsome place. But this comprised in value not more than a tenth part of his—that is, his wife's—possessions. Why should he not let or, still better, sell it, and at once and forever leave Brentville? There were no friendly ties to sunder. He was not popular in the village, and he knew it. He was popularly regarded as an interloper, who had no business with the property of which he had usurped the charge. Neither was

Roland liked, as much on his own account as on his father's, for he strutted about the village, turning up his nose at boys who would have been better off than himself in a worldly point of view but for his father's lucky marriage, and declining to engage in any game in which the first place was not accorded to him.

It was very different with Oliver. He was born to be popular. Though he possessed his share of pride, doubtless, he never showed it in an offensive manner. No poor boy ever felt ill at ease in his company. He was the life and soul of the playground, though he obtained an easy pre-eminence in the school-room.

"Oliver is worth a dozen of Roland!" was the common remark. "What a pity he was left dependent on his step-father!"

The last remark was often made to Oliver himself, but it was a subject which he was not willing to discuss. It seemed to him that he would be reproaching his mother, to find fault with the provision she had made for his future.

It did seem to him, however, in his secret heart, that his mother had been misled by too blind a confidence in his step-father.

"I wish she had left me only one-quarter of the property, and left it independent of him," he thought more than once. "She couldn't know how disagreeable it would be to me to be dependent upon him."

Oliver thought this, but he did not say it.

The thought came to him again as he walked home from the house of Frank Dudley, twenty minutes after Roland had travelled over the same road.

"I wonder whether Mr. Kenyon will be up," he asked himself, as he rang the bell. "If he is, I suppose I must make up my mind for another volley. How different it was when my poor mother was alive!"

The door was opened by Maggie, the servant.

"Has Roland come home?" he asked.

"Yes, Mr. Oliver; he is in bed by this time."

"That's good!" thought Oliver. "Is Mr. Kenyon up?"

"No, Mr. Oliver. Did you wish to see him?"

"Oh, no," said Oliver, feeling relieved. "I only enquired out of curiosity. You'd better shut up the house, Maggie."

"I was going to, Mr. Oliver."

Oliver took his lamp and went up slowly to bed. His room was just opposite to Roland's, which adjoined the apartment occupied by his father.

Remembering the scene of the previous day, Oliver expected it would be renewed when he met his stepfather and Roland at breakfast in the morning. Such, also, was the expectation of Roland. He wanted Oliver to be humiliated, and fully anticipated that he would be.

What, then, was the surprise of the two boys when Mr. Kenyon displayed an unusually gracious manner at table!

CHAPTER VI.

MR. KENYON'S CHANGE OF BASE.

"GOOD-MORNING, Oliver," he said pleasantly, when our hero entered the room.

"Good-morning, sir," returned Oliver in surprise.

"We missed you at supper last evening," continued the step-father.

"Yes, sir; I took supper at Dr. Dudley's," explained Oliver, not quite certain whether this would be considered satisfactory.

"Dr. Dudley is a very worthy man," said Mr. Kenyon. "His son is about your age, is he not?"

"Yes, sir."

"He has a daughter, also—rather a pretty girl."

"I believe Roland thinks so," said Oliver, glancing at his step-brother.

"Roland has taste, then," said Mr. Kenyon. "You two boys mustn't quarrel about the young lady."

"I shan't quarrel," said Roland stiffly. "There are plenty other girls in this world."

"You are a philosopher, I see," said his father.

Roland felt that this had gone far enough. Why should his father talk pleasantly to Oliver, who had defied his authority the day before? If this went on, Oliver would be encouraged in his insubordination. He felt that it was necessary to revive the subject.

"I expect my ball is lost," he said in an aggrieved tone.

"What ball?" asked his father.

"The ball I batted out into the road yesterday afternoon."

"Probably someone has picked it up," said Mr. Kenyon, proceeding to open an egg.

Roland was provoked at his father's coolness and unconcern.

"If Oliver had picked it up for me it would not have been lost," he continued, with a scowl at our hero.

"If you had picked it up yourself, wouldn't it have answered the same purpose ? "

Roland stared at his father in anger and dismay. Could he really mean it ? Had he been won over to Oliver's side ? Oliver, too, was surprised. He began to entertain a much more favorable opinion of his step-father.

"Didn't you tell Oliver to pick it up yesterday afternoon ? " demanded Roland, making a charge upon his father.

"Yes, I believe I did."

"Well, he didn't do it."

"He was wrong, then," said Mr. Kenyon mildly. "He should have respected my authority."

"I'll go and look for it directly breakfast is over," said Oliver, quite won over by Mr. Kenyon's mildness.

"It wouldn't be any use," said Roland. "I've been looking for it myself this morning, and it isn't there."

"Of course, it wouldn't stay there all night," said Mr. Kenyon. "It has, no doubt, been picked up."

"Aint you going to punish Oliver for disobeying you?" burst out the disappointed Roland.

Oliver turned to his step-father with interest to hear his answer.

"No, Roland. On second thought, I don't think it was his place to go for the ball. You should have gone after it yourself."

Oliver smiled to himself with secret satisfaction. He had never thought so well of his step-father before. He even felt better disposed toward Roland.

"Why didn't you ask me politely, Roland?" he said. "Then we should have saved all this trouble."

"Because I am older than you, and you ought to obey me."

"I can't agree with you there," said Oliver composedly.

"Come, boys, I can't allow any quarrelling at the table," said Mr. Kenyon, but still pleasantly. "I don't see why we can't live together in peace and quietness."

"If he will only be like that all the time," thought Oliver, "there will be some pleasure

4

in living with him. I am only afraid it won't
last. What a difference there is between his
manner to-day and yesterday."

Oliver was destined to be still more astonished when breakfast was over.

He had known for some time that Roland
was better supplied with money than himself.
In fact, he had been pinched for the want of a
little ready money more than once, and whenever he applied to Mr. Kenyon, he was either
refused or the favor was grudgingly accorded.
To-day, as he rose from the table, Mr. Kenyon
asked:

"How are you off for pocket-money,
Oliver?"

"I have twenty-five cents in my pocket,"
said Oliver with a smile.

"Then it is about time for a new supply?"

"If you please, sir."

Mr. Kenyon took a five-dollar bill from his
pocket, and passed it over to our hero.

"Thank you, sir," said Oliver, with mingled surprise and gratitude.

"How much did you give him?" asked
Roland crossly.

"The same that I give you, my son ;" and Mr. Kenyon produced another bill.

Roland took the bill discontentedly. He was not satisfied to receive no more than Oliver.

"I think," he said to our hero, "you ought to buy me a new ball out of your money."

Oliver did not reply, but looked toward Mr. Kenyon.

"I will buy you a new ball myself," he said. "There is no call for Oliver to buy one, unless he wants one for his own use."

"If you will excuse me, sir," said Oliver respectfully, "I will get ready to go to school."

"Certainly, Oliver."

Roland and his father were left alone.

"It seems to me you've taken a great fancy to Oliver all at once," said Roland.

"What makes you think so?"

"You take his part against me. Didn't you tell him yesterday to go after my ball?"

"Yes."

"To-day you blame me for not going my-self. You reward him for his impudence besides by giving him five dollars."

Mr. Kenyon smiled.

"So my conduct puzzles you, does it?" he inquired complacently.

"Yes, it does. I should think Oliver was your son instead of me."

"Have I not treated you as well as Oliver?"

"I think you ought to treat me better, considering I am your own son," grumbled Roland.

"I have good reasons for my conduct," said Mr. Kenyon mysteriously.

"What are they?"

"You are a boy, and it is not fitting I should tell you everything."

"You aint afraid of Oliver, are you?" demanded Roland bluntly.

Mr. Kenyon smiled pleasantly, showing a set of very white teeth as he did so.

"Really, that is amusing," he answered. "What on earth should make me afraid of Oliver?"

"I don't see what other reason you can have for backing down as you have."

"Listen, Roland. There is more than one

way of arriving at a result, but there is always one way that is wiser than any other. Now it would not be wise for me to treat Oliver in such a way as to create unfavorable comment in the village."

"What do you care for what people in the village think?" asked Roland bluntly. "Haven't you got the money?"

"Yes."

"And Oliver hasn't a cent?"

"He has nothing except what I choose to give him."

"Good!" said Roland with satisfaction. "I hope you don't mean to give him as much as you do me," he added.

"Not in the end. Just at present I may."

"I don't see why you should."

"Then you must be content to take my word for it, and trust to my judgment. In the end you may be assured that I shall look out for your interests, and that you will be far better off than Oliver."

With this promise Roland was measurably satisfied. The thing that troubled him was that Oliver seemed to have triumphed over him in their recent little difference. Perhaps, could he have fathomed his step-father's secret designs respecting Oliver, he would have felt less dissatisfied. Mr. Kenyon was never more to be dreaded than when he protessed to be friendly.

CHAPTER VII.

ROLAND'S DISCOMFITURE.

ON the way to school Oliver overtook Frank Dudley.

"Well, Oliver, how's the weather at home?" asked Frank. "Cloudy, eh?"

"No; it's all clear and serene."

Frank looked astonished.

"Didn't Mr. Kenyon blow you up, then?" he asked.

"Not a bit of it. He gave me a five-dollar bill without my asking for it."

"What's come over him?" asked Frank in amazement. "His mind isn't getting affected, is it?"

Oliver laughed.

"Not that I know of," he said. "I don't wonder you ask. I never saw such a change come over a man since yesterday. Then he wanted Roland to flog me. Now he is like an indulgent parent."

"It's queer, decidedly. I hope, for your sake, it 'll hold out."

"So do I. Roland doesn't seem to fancy it, though. He tried hard to revive the quarrel of yesterday, but without success."

"He's an amiable cub, that Roland."

"Do you speak thus of your future brother-in-law?"

"Carrie would sooner be an old maid a dozen times over than give any encouragement to such a fellow."

All of which was pleasant for Oliver to hear.

Mr. Kenyon was not through with his surprises.

Two weeks before, Roland had a new suit of clothes. Oliver's envy had been a little excited, because he needed new clothes more than his step-brother, but he was too proud to give expression to his dissatisfaction or to ask for a similar favor. On the way home from school, in company with Frank Dudley, Oliver met Mr. Kenyon.

"Are you just coming home from school, Oliver?" asked his step-father pleasantly.

"Yes, sir."

"I have told Mr. Crimp, the tailor, to measure you for a new suit of clothes. You may as well call in now and be measured."

"Thank you, sir," said Oliver, in a tone of satisfaction.

What boy ever was indifferent to new clothes?

"Have you selected the cloth, sir?" he asked.

"No; you may make the selection yourself. You need not regard the price. It is best to get a good article."

Mr. Kenyon waved his hand, and smiling pleasantly, walked away.

"Look here, Oliver," said Frank, "I begin to think you have misrepresented Mr. Kenyon to me. Such a man as that tyrannical! Why, he looks as if butter wouldn't melt in his mouth."

"I don't know what to make of it myself, Frank. I never saw such a change in a man, If he'll keep on treating me like this I shall really begin to like him. Will you come to the tailor's with me?"

"Willingly. It 'll be the next thing to ordering a suit for myself."

The tailor's shop was near by, and the boys entered, with their school-books in their hands.

Oliver, with his friend's approval, selected a piece of expensive cloth, and was measured for a suit. As they left the shop they fell in with Roland, who, cane in hand, was walking leisurely down the main street, cherishing the complacent delusion that he was the object of general admiration.

"Hallo, Frank!" he said, by way of greeting. To Oliver he did not vouchsafe a word.

Frank Dudley nodded.

"Are you out for a walk?" he added.

"Yes."

"Have you been into Crimp's?"

"Yes."

"Been ordering new clothes?" enquired Roland, with interest, for he was rather a dandy, and was as much interested in clothes as a lady.

"I haven't. Oliver has."

Roland arched his brows in displeasure.

"Have you ordered a suit of clothes?" he enquired.

"I have," answered Oliver coldly.

"Who authorized you to do it?"

"It is none of your business," said Oliver, justly provoked at the other's impertinence.

"It is my father's business," said Roland. "I suppose you expect to pay for them."

"The bill won't be sent to you, at any rate. You may be assured of that. Come on, Frank."

The two boys walked off, leaving Roland in front of the tailor's shop.

"I'll go in and see what he's ordered," thought he. "If it's without authority I'll tell my father, and he'll soon put a spoke in his wheel."

"Good-evening, Crimp," said he consequentially.

Considering the tailor quite beneath him he dispensed with any title.

"Good-evening," returned the tailor.

"Oliver has ordered a suit here, hasn't he?"

"Yes; he just ordered it."

" Will you show me the cloth he selected ?"

" If you wish."

Mr. Crimp displayed the cloth. Roland was enough of a judge to see that it was high priced.

" It's nice cloth.   Is it expensive ?"

" It's the best I have in stock."

Roland frowned.

" Is it any better than the suit you made me a short time since ? "

" It is a little dearer."

" Why didn't you show me this, then?   I wanted the best."

" Because it has come in since."

" Look here, Crimp," said Roland, " you'd better wait till you hear from my father before you begin on this suit."

" Why should I ? "

" I don't believe he will allow Oliver to have such a high-priced suit."

Mr. Crimp had had orders from Mr. Kenyon that very afternoon to follow Oliver's direc-tions implicitly, but he did not choose to say this to Roland.   The truth was, he was pro-voked at the liberty the ill-bred boy took in addressing him without a title, and he didn't see fit to enlighten him on this point.

"You must excuse me," he said. "Oliver has ordered the suit, and I shall not take such a liberty with him as to question his order."

"I rather think my father will have something to say about that," said Roland. "I presume you expect him to pay your bill."

"The bill will be paid; I am not afraid of that. Why shouldn't it be?"

"You may have to depend on Oliver to pay it himself."

"Well, he has money enough, or ought to have," said the tailor significantly. "His mother left a large property."

Roland did not like the turn the conversation was taking, and stalked out of the shop.

"Crimp is getting impudent," he said to himself. "If there was another good tailor in the village I would patronize him."

However, Roland had one other resource, and this consoled him.

"I'll tell my father, and we'll see if he don't put a stop to it," he thought. "Oliver will find he can't do just as he likes. I wish Crimp

would make the suit, and then father refuse
to pay for it. It would teach him a lesson."

Roland selected the supper-table for the
revelation of what he supposed to be Oliver's
unauthorized conduct.

"I met Oliver coming out of Crimp's this
afternoon," he commenced.

Oliver did not appear alarmed at this
opening. He continued to eat his toast in
silence.

As no one said anything, Roland continued :

"He had just been ordering a new suit of
clothes."

"Did you find any cloth to suit you,
Oliver?" asked Mr. Kenyon.

"Yes, sir, I found a very nice piece."

"I should think it was nice. It was the
dearest in Crimp's stock!" said Roland.

"How do you know?" asked Oliver
quickly.

"Crimp told me so."

"Then you went in and enquired," said
Oliver, his lip curling.

"Yes, I did."

"I am glad you selected a good article,

Oliver," said Mr. Kenyon quietly. "It will wear longer."

Roland stared at his father in open-mouthed amazement. He so fully anticipated getting Oliver into hot water that his father quite disconcerted him.

"His suit is going to be better than mine," he grumbled, in a tone of vexation.

"That is your own fault. Why didn't you select the same cloth?" asked his father.

"It is some new cloth that has just come in."

"You can make it up next time," said Mr. Kenyon; "your suit seems to me to be a very nice one."

This was all the satisfaction Roland got.

The next day he met Mr. Crimp in the street.

"Well, does your father object to Oliver's order?" he asked with a smile.

Roland was too provoked to notice what he regarded as an impertinent question.

CHAPTER VIII.

A DANGEROUS LETTER.

THERE are some men who seem to be utterly destitute of principle. These are the men who in cold blood show themselves guilty of the most appalling crimes if their interest requires it. They are more detestable than those who, a prey to strong passion, are hurried into the commission of acts which in their cooler moments they deeply regret.

To the first class belonged Mr. Kenyon, who, as we have already seen, had committed his wife to the horrible confinement of a mad-house that he might be free to spend her fortune. Hitherto he had not injured Oliver, though he had made his life uncomfortable; but the time was coming when our hero would be himself in peril. It was because he foresaw that Oliver might need to be removed that he began to treat him with unusual indulgence.

"Should anything happen," he said to himself, "this will disarm suspicion."

The time came sooner than he anticipated. Action was precipitated by a most unlooked for occurrence, which filled the soul of the guilty husband with terror.

One day he stopped at the post-office to enquire for letters.

"There is no letter for you, Mr. Kenyon, but here is one for Oliver. Will you take it?"

Mr. Kenyon was curious to learn with whom his step-son corresponded, and said:

"Yes, I will take it."

It was put into his hands. No sooner did he scan the handwriting and the postmark than he turned actually livid.

It was in the handwriting of his wife, whom all the world supposed to be dead, and it was postmarked Charleston.

"Good Heavens! What a narrow escape!" he ejaculated, the perspiration standing in large drops on his brow. "Suppose Oliver had received this letter, I might have been

5

lynched. I must go home and consider what is to be done. How could Dr. Fox be so criminally—idiotically careless as to suffer such a letter to leave his establishment?"

Mr. Kenyon hurried home, much perturbed.

On the way he met Roland, who could not help observing his father's agitation.

"What is the matter, father?" he enquired carelessly, for he cared very little for anyone but himself.

"I have a sick headache," said his father abruptly. "I am going home to lie down."

Roland made no further enquiries, and Mr. Kenyon gained the house without any other encounter.

He went up to his own room and locked himself in. Then he took out his pocket-knife and cut open the envelope. The letter was as follows:

MY DEAR OLIVER:

This letter is from your unhappy mother, who is languishing in a private mad-house, the victim of your step-father's detestable machinations. Oh, Oliver, how can I reveal to you the hypocrisy and the baseness of that man, whom in an evil hour I accepted as the successor of your dear father. It was not because I loved him, but rather because of his importunity, that I yielded my assent to his proposals. I did not know his character then. I did not know, as I do now, that he only wanted to secure my property. He professed himself to be wealthy, but I have reason to think that in this, as in other things, he deceived me.

When we came South he pretended that it was on account of his health, and I unsuspectingly fell into the snare. I need not dwell upon the details of that journey. Enough that he lured me here and placed me under the charge of a Dr. Fox, a fitting tool of his, under the plea that I was insane.

I am given to understand that on his return to the North Mr. Kenyon represented me as dead. Such is his art that I do not doubt his story has been believed. Perhaps you, my dearest son, have mourned for me as dead. If this be so, my letter will be a revelation. I have been trying for a long time to get an opportunity to write you, but this is the first time I have met with success. I do not yet know if I can get it safely to the mail, but that is my hope.

When you receive this letter consult with friends whom you can trust, and be guided by their advice. Do what you can to rescue me from this living death. Do not arouse the suspicions of Mr. Kenyon if you can avoid it. He is capable of anything.

My dear son, my paper is exhausted, and I dare not write more, at any rate, lest I should be interrupted and detected. Heaven bless you and restore you to my longing sight.

Your loving mother,

MARGARET CONRAD.

Mr. Kenyon's face darkened, especially when his attention was drawn to the signature.

"Conrad! So she discards my name!" he muttered. "Fortunately the object of this accursed letter will not be attained, nor will Oliver have an opportunity of making mischief by showing it to the neighbors."

Mr. Kenyon lighted a candle and deliberately held the dangerous letter in the flame till it was consumed.

"There," he said, breathing a sigh of relief, "that peril is over. But suppose she should write another?"

Again his face wore an expression of nervous apprehension.

"I must write to Dr. Fox at once," he mused, "and warn him to keep close guard over his patient. Otherwise I may have to dread an explosion at any time."

He threw himself into an easy chair and began to think over the situation.

The man was alert and watchful. Danger was at hand, and he resolved to head it off at any hazard.

Meanwhile Oliver had occasion to pass the

post-office on his way home from school. Thinking there might be a letter or paper for his step-father, he entered and made enquiry.

"Is there anything for us, Mr. Herman?" he said.

"No," said the postmaster, adding jocularly: "Isn't one letter a day enough for you?"

"I have received no letter," answered Oliver, rather surprised.

"I gave a letter to Mr. Kenyon for you this morning."

"Oh, I haven't been home from school yet," said Oliver. "I suppose it is waiting for me there."

"Very likely. It looked to be in a lady's handwriting," added the postmaster, disposed to banter Oliver, who was a favorite with him.

"I can't think who can have written it, then," said our hero.

At first he thought it might be from an intimate boy friend of about his own age, but the postmaster's remark seemed to render that unlikely.

We all like to receive letters, however disinclined we may be to answer them. Oliver was no exception in this respect. His desire to see the letter was increased by his being quite unable to conjecture who could have written to him in a feminine handwriting. As soon, therefore, as he reached home, he enquired for Mr. Kenyon.

"He's in his room, Mr. Oliver," said the servant.

"Did he leave any letter for me, Maggie?"

"I didn't hear of any, Mr. Oliver."

"Then he's got it upstairs, I suppose."

Oliver went up the stairs and knocked at Mr. Kenyon's door. The latter had now recovered his wonted composure, and called out to him to enter.

"I heard you had a letter for me, Mr. Kenyon," said Oliver abruptly.

Again Mr. Kenyon looked disturbed. He had hoped that Oliver would hear nothing of it, and that no enquiry might be made.

"Who told you I had a letter for you?"

"The postmaster."

Mr. Kenyon saw that it was useless to deny it.

"Yes, I believe there was one," he said carelessly. "Where could I have put it?"

He began to search his pockets; then he looked into the drawers of his desk.

"I don't remember laying it down," he said slowly. "In fact, I don't remember seeing it since I got home. I may have dropped it in the road."

"Won't you oblige me by looking again, sir?" asked Oliver, disappointed.

Mr. Kenyon looked again, but, of course, in vain.

"It may turn up," he said at length. "Not that it was of any importance. It looked like a circular."

"Mr. Herman told me it was in feminine handwriting," said Oliver.

"Oho! that accounts for your anxiety!" said Mr. Kenyon, with affected jocularity. "Come, I'll look again."

But the letter was not found.

Oliver did not fail to notice something singular in his step-father's manner.

"Has he suppressed my letter?" he asked himself, as he slowly retired from the room. "What does it all mean?"

"He suspects me," muttered Mr. Kenyon. "He is in my way, and I must get rid of him."

CHAPTER IX.

OLIVER'S MOTHER.

IT is time to introduce Oliver's mother, who was suffering such cruel imprisonment within the walls of a mad-house.

It was by a subterfuge she had first been induced to enter the asylum of Dr. Fox. Her husband had spoken of it as a boarding-school under the charge of an old friend of his.

"I think, my dear," he said, as they dismounted at the gate, "that you will be interested to look over the institution, and I know it will afford my friend great pleasure to show it to you."

"I dare say I shall find it interesting," she answered, and they entered.

Dr. Fox met them at the door. He had received previous notice of their arrival, and a bargain had been struck between Mr. Kenyon and the doctor. A meaning look was exchanged between them which Mrs. Kenyon did not notice.

"I have brought my wife to look over your establishment, doctor," said Mr. Kenyon.

"I don't think it is worth looking at," said the doctor, "but I shall be very glad to show it. Will you come upstairs?"

They were moving up the main staircase when a loud scream was heard from above, proceeding from one of the insane inmates.

"What is that?" asked Mrs. Kenyon, stopping short and turning pale.

Mr. Kenyon bit his lip. He feared that his wife would suspect too soon the character of the institution. But Dr. Fox was prepared for the question.

"It is poor Tommy Briggs," he said, shrugging his shoulders. "He is in the sickward."

"But what is the matter with him?" asked Mrs. Kenyon, shuddering as another wild shriek was borne to her ears.

"He has fits," answered the doctor.

"Ought he to be here, then?"

"He has them only at intervals, say once

a month.   To-morrow he will be all right
again."

Mrs. Kenyon accepted this explanation
without suspicion.

" How old is he ? " she asked.

" Fifteen."

" About the age of Oliver," she remarked,
turning to her husband.

" Or Roland."

" What a misfortune it must be to have a
boy so afflicted ! How I pity his poor mother ! "

" Come up another flight, please," said
Dr. Fox.   " We will begin our examination
there."

They went up to the next story.

Dr. Fox drew a bunch of keys from his
pocket, and applying one to the door opened it.

" Do you keep them locked in ? " asked Mrs.
Kenyon, surprised.

" This is one of the dormitories," answered
the doctor, who never lost his self-possession.
" Come in, please."

It was a large square room. In one corner
was a bed, surrounded by curtains. In the
opposite corner was another bed—a cot.

" Sit down one moment, Mrs. Kenyon," said
the doctor.   " I want to call a servant."

He left the room, and Mr. Kenyon followed him.

The two men regarded each other with a
complacent smile.

" Well, it's done," said the doctor, rubbing
his hands.   " She walked into the trap without any suspicion or fuss."

" You'd better lock the door," said Mr.
Kenyon nervously.

The doctor did so.

" Now," said he, " if you will follow me
downstairs we will attend to the business part
of the matter."

" Willingly," said Kenyon.

The business referred to consisted of the
payment of three months' board in advance.

" Now, Dr. Fox," said his new patron,
" you may rely upon punctual payment of
your bills.   On your part, I depend on your
safe custody of my wife as long as her mind
remains unsound."

" And that will be a long time, I fancy,"
said the doctor, laughing.

Mr. Kenyon appreciated the joke, and laughed too.

"I must leave you now," he said. "I hope you won't have much trouble with her."

"Oh, have no anxiety on that score," said the doctor nonchalantly. "I am used to such cases; I know how to manage."

The two men shook hands, and Mr. Kenyon left the asylum a free man.

"So far, well," he said, when he was in the open air. "At last—at last, I am rich! And I mean to enjoy my wealth!"

Mrs. Kenyon remained in the seat assigned her for two or three minutes. Then she began to wonder why her husband and the doctor did not return.

"It's strange they leave me here so long," she said to herself.

Then she rose and went to the door.

She tried to open it, but it resisted her efforts.

"What does this mean?" she asked herself, bewildered.

She turned, and was startled by seeing a tall

woman, in a long calico robe, in the act of emerging from the curtained bed. The woman had long hair, which, unconfined, descended over her shoulders. Her features wore a strange look, which startled and alarmed Mrs. Kenyon.

"How did you get into my room?" asked the woman sharply.

"Is this your room?" asked Mrs. Kenyon, unable to remove her eyes from the strange apparition.

"Yes, it is my audience chamber," was the reply. "Why are you here?"

"I hardly know," said Mrs. Kenyon hurriedly. "I think there must be some mistake. I would go out if I could, but the door is locked."

"They always lock it," said the other composedly.

"Do you live here?" asked Mrs. Kenyon nervously.

"Oh, yes, I have lived here for five hundred years, more or less."

"What!" exclaimed Mrs. Kenyon, terror-stricken.

"I said more or less," repeated the woman sharply. "How can I tell within fifty years? Do you know who I am?"

"No."

"You have often heard of me," said the other complacently. "The whole world has heard about me. I am Queen Cleopatra."

Mrs. Kenyon knew where she was now. She realized it with a heart full of horror. But what could it mean? Could Mr. Kenyon have left her there intentionally? In spite of all she had learned about it she could hardly credit it.

"What place is this, tell me?" she implored.

"I'll tell you," said the woman, "but you mustn't tell," she added, with a look of cunning. "I've found it all out. It's a place where they send crazy people."

"Good Heaven!"

"They are all crazy here—all but me," continued Cleopatra, to call her by the name she assumed. "I am only here for my health," she continued. "That's what the doctor tells me, though why they should keep me so long

I cannot understand. Sometimes I suspect——"

"In Heaven's name, what?"

The woman advanced toward Mrs. Kenyon, who shrank from her instinctively, and whispered :

"They want to separate me and Mark Antony," she said. "I am convinced of it, though whether it's Cæsar or my ministers who have done it I can't tell. What do you think?" she demanded, fixing her eyes searchingly upon Mrs. Kenyon.

"I don't know," answered Mrs. Kenyon, shrinking away from her.

"You needn't be afraid of me," said Cleopatra, observing the movement. "I am not crazy, you know. I am perfectly harmless. Are you crazy?"

"Heaven forbid!" exclaimed Mrs. Kenyon with a shudder.

"They all say so," said Cleopatra shrewdly, "but they are all crazy except me. Do you hear that?"

There was another wild shriek, proceeding from a room on the same floor.

" Who is it ? " asked Mrs. Kenyon, in alarm.

"It's crazy Nancy," answered Cleopatra. " She thinks she's the wife of Henry VIII., and she is always afraid he will have her executed. It's queer what fancies these people have," added Cleopatra, laughing.

" How unconscious she is of her infirmity ! " thought Mrs. Kenyon. " I hope she's never violent."

" Is there a bell here ? " she asked.

" What for ? "

" I wish to ring for the doctor and my husband."

" Ho ! ho ! Do you think they would notice your ringing ? "

" Do you think they mean to leave me here ? " asked Mrs. Kenyon, with a gasp of horror.

" To be sure they do. The doctor told me this morning he was going to give me a nice, agreeable room-mate."

The full horror of her situation was revealed to the unfortunate woman, and she sank upon the floor in a swoon

CHAPTER X

WHEN Mrs. Kenyon recovered from her swoon, she saw Dr. Fox bending over her.

"You are recovering," he said. "You mustn't give way like this, my good madam."

It all came back to her—her desertion, and the terrible imprisonment which awaited her.

"Where is my husband—where is Mr. Kenyon?" she demanded imperatively.

Dr. Fox shrugged his shoulders.

"I wish you to send him here at once, or to take me to him."

"Quite impossible, my dear madam. He has gone."

"Mr. Kenyon gone, and left me here!"

"It is for your own good, my dear madam. I hope soon to restore you to him."

It was as she expected, and the first shock

being over, she took the announcement calmly. But her soul was stirred with anger and resentment, for she was a woman of spirit.

"This is all a base plot," she said scornfully. "Has Mr. Kenyon—have you—the assurance to assert that my mind is disordered?"

"Unhappily there is no doubt of it," said the doctor, in a tone of affected regret. "Your present excitement shows it."

"My excitement! Who would not be excited at being entrapped in such a way? But I quite comprehend Mr. Kenyon's motives. How much does he pay you for your share in this conspiracy?"

"He pays your board on my usual terms," said Dr. Fox composedly. "I have agreed to do my best to cure you of your unhappy malady, but I can do little while you suffer yourself to become so excited."

His tone was significant, and contained a menace, but for this Mrs. Kenyon cared little. She had been blind, but she was clear-sighted now. She felt that it was her husband's

object to keep her in perpetual imprisonment. Thus only could his ends be attained.

She was silent for a moment. She perceived that craft must be met with craft, and
that it was best to control her excitement.
She would speak her mind, however, to avoid
being misunderstood.

"I will not judge you, Dr. Fox," she said.
"Possibly Mr. Kenyon may have deceived
you for his own purposes. If you are really
skilled in mental diseases you will soon perceive that I am as sane as you are yourself."

"When I make that discovery I will send
you back to your husband," said the doctor
with oily suavity.

"I shall never return to my husband," said
Mrs. Kenyon coldly. "I only ask to be released. I hope your promise is made in good
faith."

"Certainly it is ; but, my dear madam, let
me beg you to lay aside this prejudice against
your husband, who sincerely regrets the necessity of your temporary seclusion from the
world."

Mrs. Kenyon smiled bitterly.

"I understand Mr. Kenyon probably better than you do," she said. "We won't discuss him now. But if I am to remain here, even for a short time, I have a favor to ask."

"You may ask it, certainly," said the doctor, who did not, however, couple with the permission any promise to grant the request.

"Or, rather, I have two requests to make," said Mrs. Kenyon.

"Name them."

"The first is, to be supplied with pens, ink, and paper, that I may communicate with **my** friends."

"Meaning your husband?"

"He is not my friend, but I shall address one letter to him."

"Very well. You shall have what you require. You can hand the letters to me, and I will have them posted."

"You will not read them?"

"It is our usual rule to read all letters written from this establishment, but in your case we will waive the rule, and allow them to go unread. What is your second request?"

"I should like a room alone," said Mrs.

Kenyon, glancing at Cleopatra, who was sitting on the side of the bed listening to the conversation.

"I am sorry that I can't grant that request," said the doctor. "The fact is, my establishment is too full to give anyone a single room."

"But you won't keep me in the same room with a——"

"What do you call me?" interrupted Cleopatra angrily. "Do you mean to say I am crazy? You ought to feel proud of having the Queen of Egypt for a room-mate. I will make you the Mistress of the Robes."

All this was ludicrous enough, considering the shabby attire of the self-styled queen, but Mrs. Kenyon did not feel in a laughing humor. She did not reply, but glanced meaningly at the door.

"I am sure you will like Cleopatra," he said, adding, with a wink unobserved by the Egyptian sovereign, "she is the only sane person in my establishment."

Cleopatra nodded in a tone of satisfaction.

"You hear what he says?" she said, turning to Mrs. Kenyon.

The latter saw that it was not wise to provoke one who would probably be her roommate.

"I don't object to her," she said ; "but to anyone. Give me any room, however small, so that I occupy it alone."

"Impossible, my dear madam," said her keeper decisively. "I can assure you that Cleopatra, though confined here for political reasons," here he bowed to the royal lunatic, "never gives any trouble, but is quite calm and patient."

"Thank you, doctor," said Cleopatra. "You understand me. Did you forward my last letter to Mark Antony?"

"Yes, your Majesty. I have no doubt he will answer it as soon as his duties in the field will permit."

"Where is he now?"

"I think he is heading an expedition somewhere in Asia Minor."

"Very well," nodded Cleopatra. "As soon as a letter comes, send it to me."

"At once," said the doctor. "You must look after this lady, and cheer her up."

"Yes, I will.   What is your name?"

"My name used to be Conrad. You may call me that."

She shrank from wearing the name of the man who had confined her in this terrible asylum.

"That isn't classical.   I will call you Claudia—may I?"

"You may call me anything you like," said Mrs. Kenyon wearily.

"When will you send me the paper and ink?" she asked.

"They shall be sent up at once."

Ten minutes later, writing materials were brought.   Anxious to do something which might lead to her release, she sat down and wrote letters to two gentlemen of influence with whom she was acquainted, giving the details of the plot which had been so successfully carried out against her liberty.

Cleopatra watched her curiously.   Presently she said:

"Will you let me have a sheet of your paper? I wish to write a letter to Mark Antony."

"Certainly," said Mrs. Kenyon, regarding her with pity and sympathy.

The other seated herself and wrote rapidly, in an elegant feminine hand, which surprised Mrs. Kenyon. She did not know that the poor lady had once been classical teacher in a prominent female seminary, and that it was a disappointment in love which had alienated her mind and reduced her to her present condition.

"Shall I read you the letter?" she enquired.

"If you like."

It was a very well written appeal to her imaginary correspondent to hasten to her and restore her to her throne.

"I thought," said Mrs. Kenyon cautiously, "that Mark Antony died many centuries ago."

"Quite a mistake, I assure you. Who could have told you such nonsense, Claudia?" demanded Cleopatra sharply.

"You are quite sure, then?"

"Of course. You will begin to say next that Cleopatra is dead."

"I thought so."

"That is because I have remained here so long in concealment. The world supposes me dead, but the time will come when people will learn their mistake. Have you finished your letters?"

"Yes."

"When they send us our supper you can send them to the doctor."

"Will he be sure to post them?" asked Mrs. Kenyon, with a natural suspicion.

"Of course. Doesn't he always send my letters to Mark Antony?"

This was not as satisfactory as it might have been.

"Have you ever received any answers?" asked Mrs. Kenyon.

"Here is a letter from Mark Antony," said Cleopatra, taking a dirty and crumpled note from her pocket. "Read it, Claudia."

This was the note:

FAIR CLEOPATRA:
I have read your letter, my heart's sovereign, and I kiss the hand that wrote it. I am driving the enemy before me, and hope soon to kneel before

you, crowned with laurels. Be patient, and soon expect your captive,

MARK ANTONY.

"Is it not a beautiful letter?" asked Cleopatra proudly.

"Yes," said Mrs. Kenyon, feeling it best to humor her delusion.

CHAPTER XI.

SEVERAL months passed, and Mrs. Kenyon remained in confinement. She was not badly treated, except in being vigilantly guarded, and prevented from making her escape. Dr. Fox always treated her with suavity, but she felt that though covered with velvet his hand was of iron, and that there was little to hope for from him. He never made any objection to her writing letters, but always insisted on their being handed to him.

It was not long before she began seriously to doubt whether the letters thus committed to him were really mailed, since no answers came. One day she asked him abruptly:

"Why is it, Dr. Fox, that I get no answers to my letters?"

"I suppose," he answered, "that your friends are afraid you may be excited, and

92

your recovery retarded, by hearing from them."

"Has my—has Mr. Kenyon reported that I am insane?"

"Undoubtedly."

"False and treacherous!" she exclaimed bitterly. "Why was I ever mad enough to marry him?"

Dr. Fox shrugged his shoulders.

"Really," he said, "I couldn't pretend to explain your motives, my dear madam. Women are enigmas."

"Are my letters regularly mailed, Dr. Fox?" asked Mrs. Kenyon searchingly.

"How can you ask such a question? Do you not commit them to me?"

"So does Cleopatra," said Mrs. Kenyon, who had fallen into the habit of addressing her room-mate by the name she assumed. "Do you forward her letters to Mark Antony?"

"Does she doubt it?" asked the doctor, bowing to the mad queen.

"No, doctor," replied Cleopatra promptly. "I have the utmost faith in your loyality, and it shall be rewarded. I have long intended to make you Lord High Baron of the Nile. Let this be the emblem."

In a dignified manner Cleopatra advanced toward Dr. Fox, and passed a bit of faded ribbon through his button-hole.

"Thanks, your Majesty," said the doctor. "Your confidence is not misplaced. I will keep this among my chief treasures."

Cleopatra looked pleased, and Mrs. Kenyon impatient and disgusted.

"He deceives me as he does her, without doubt. It is useless to question him further."

From this time she sedulously watched for an opportunity to write a letter and commit it to other hands than the doctor's. But, that he might not suspect her design, she also wrote regularly, and placed the letters in his hands.

One day the opportunity came. A young man, related to Cleopatra, visited the institution. He understood very well the character of his aunt's aberration, but was surprised to be told that the quiet lady who bore her company was also crazy.

"What is the nature of her malady?" he enquired of the doctor. "Is she ever violent?"

"Oh, no."

"She seems rational enough."

"So she is on all points except one."

"What is that?"

"She thinks her husband has confined her here in order to enjoy her property. In point of fact she has no property and no husband."

"That is curious. Why, then, does she require to be confined?"

"Probably she will soon be released. She has improved very much since she came here."

"I am glad my aunt has so quiet a companion."

"Yes, they harmonize very well. They have never disagreed."

During one of Mr. Arthur Holman's visits Mrs. Kenyon managed to slip into his hands a sealed letter.

"Will you have the kindness," she asked quickly, "to put this into the post-office without informing the doctor?"

"I will," he answered readily.

"Poor woman!" he thought to himself. "It will gratify her, and her letter will do no harm."

"I shall have to be indebted to your kindness for a postage-stamp," she said. "I cannot obtain them here."

"Oh, don't mention it," he said.

"You will be sure not to mention this to the doctor?" said Mrs Kenyon earnestly.

"On my honor as a gentleman."

"I believe you," she said quietly.

This was the letter, directed to Oliver, which found its way into the hands of Mr. Kenyon, and occasioned him so much uneasiness.

CHAPTER XII.

OLIVER'S JOURNEY.

THE more Oliver thought about it, the stranger it seemed to him that the letter intended for him should have been lost. In spite of Mr. Kenyon's plausible explanations, he felt that it had been suppressed. But why? He could conceive of no motive for the deed. He had no secret correspondent, nor had he any secret to conceal. He was quite at sea in his conjectures.

He could not help showing by his manner the suspicion he entertained. Mr. Kenyon did not appear to notice it, but it was far from escaping his attention. He knew something about character reading, and he saw that Oliver was very determined, and, once aroused, would make trouble.

"There is only one way," he muttered, as he furtively regarded the grave look on the boyish face of his step-son. "There is only one way, and I must try it!"

He felt that there was daily peril. Any day another letter might arrive at the post-office, and it might fall this time into Oliver's hands. True, he had received a letter from Dr. Fox, in which he expressed his inability to discover how the letter had been mailed without his knowledge, but assuring Mr. Kenyon that it should not happen again.

"I shall not hereafter allow your wife the use of writing materials," he said. "This will remove all danger."

Still Mr. Kenyon felt unsettled and ill at ease. In spite of all Dr. Fox's precautions, a letter might be written, and this would be most disastrous to him.

"Oliver," said Mr. Kenyon one evening, "I have to go to New York on business to-morrow; would you like to go with me?"

"Yes, sir," said Oliver promptly.

To a country boy, who had not been in New York more than half a dozen times in the course of his life, such a trip promised great enjoyment, even where the company was uncongenial.

"We shall probably remain over night," said his step-father. "I don't think I can get through all my business in one day."

"All the better, sir," said Oliver. "I never stopped over night in New York."

"Then you will enjoy it. If I have a chance I will take you to the theatre."

"Thank you, sir," said Oliver, forgetting for the moment his prejudice against his step-father. "Is Roland going?" he asked.

"No," answered Mr. Kenyon.

Oliver stared in surprise. It seemed strange to him that he should be offered an enjoyment of which Roland was deprived.

"I can't undertake to manage two boys at a time," said Mr. Kenyon decisively. "Roland will have to wait till the next time."

"That's queer," thought Oliver, but he did not dwell too much on the thought. He was too well satisfied with having been the favored one, for this time at least.

Roland was not present when his father made this proposal, but he soon heard of it.

His dissatisfaction may well be imagined. What! Was he, Mr. Kenyon's own son, to be passed over in favor of Oliver? He became alarmed. Was he losing his old place, and was Oliver going to supplant him? To his mind Oliver had of late been treated altogether too well, and he did not like it.

He rushed into his father's presence, his cheeks pale with anger.

"What is this I hear?" he burst out. "Are you going to take Oliver to New York, and leave me at home?"

"Yes, Roland, but——"

"Then it's a mean shame. Anyone would think he was your son, and not I."

"You don't understand, Roland. I have an object in view."

"What is it?" asked Roland, his curiosity overcoming his anger.

"It will be better for you in the end, Roland. You don't like Oliver, do you?"

"No. I hate him."

"You wouldn't mind if he didn't come back, would you?"

"Is that what you mean, father?" asked Roland, pricking up his ears.

"Yes. I am going to place him in a cheap boarding-school where he will be ruled with a rod of iron. Of course Oliver doesn't understand that. He thinks only that he is going to take a little trip to New York. Your presence would interfere with my plans, don't you see?"

"That's good," chuckled Roland with malicious merriment. "Do they flog at the school he's going to?"

"With great severity."

"Ho! ho! He'll get more than he bargains for. I don't mind staying at home now, father."

"Hope you'll have a good time, Oliver," said Roland, with a chuckle, when Oliver and his father were on the point of starting. "How lonely I'll feel without you!"

Oliver thought it rather strange that Roland should acquiesce so readily in the plan which left him at home, but it soon passed away from his mind.

CHAPTER XIII.

MR. KENYON'S PLANS FOR OLIVER.

SOON after they were seated in the cars, bound for New York, Mr. Kenyon remarked:

"Perhaps you are surprised, Oliver, that I take you with me instead of Roland."

Oliver admitted that he was surprised.

"The fact is," said Mr. Kenyon candidly, "I don't think Roland treats you as well as he should."

Oliver was more and more surprised.

"I don't complain of Roland," he said. "I don't think he likes me, but perhaps that is not his fault. We are quite different."

"Still he might treat you well."

"Don't think of that, Mr. Kenyon; Roland has never done me any serious harm, and if he proposed to do it, I am able to take care of myself."

Oliver did not say this in an offensive tone, but with manly independence.

"You are quite magnanimous," said Mr. Kenyon. "I am just beginning to appreciate you. I own that I used to have a prejudice against you, and it is possible I may have treated you harshly; but I have learned to know you better. I find you a straightforward, manly young fellow."

"Thank you, sir," said Oliver, very much astonished. "I am afraid you do me more than justice. I hope to retain your good opinion."

"I have no doubt you will," said Mr. Kenyon, in a quiet and paternal tone. "You have probably noticed that my manner toward you has changed of late?"

"Yes, sir, I have noticed the change, and been glad to see it."

"Of course, of course. Now, I have got something to tell you."

Oliver naturally felt curious.

"I want to tell you why I have brought you to New York to-day. You probably thought it was merely for a pleasant excursion."

"Yes, sir."

"I have another object in view. Noticing as I have the dislike—well, the incompatibility between you and Roland, I have thought it best to make separate arrangements for you."

Now Oliver was strangely interested. What plan had Mr. Kenyon formed for him?

"I intend you to remain in the city. How does that suit you?"

There are not many boys of Oliver's age to whom such a prospect would not be pleasing. He answered promptly:

"I should like it very much."

"No doubt Roland will envy you," said Mr. Kenyon. "I am sure he would prefer the city to our quiet little country village. But I cannot make up my mind to part with him. He is my own son, and though I endeavor to treat you both alike, of course that makes some difference," said Mr. Kenyon, in rather an apologetic tone.

"Of course it does," said Oliver, who did not feel in the least sensitive about his step-father's superior affection for Roland.

"Where am I to live in the city?" he asked next.

"There are two courses open to you," said Mr. Kenyon. "You might either go to some school in the city or enter some place of business. Which would you prefer?"

Had Oliver been an enthusiastic student, he would have decided in favor of school. He was a good scholar for his age, but, like all boys, he fancied a change. It seemed to him that he would like to obtain a business position, and he said so.

His step-father anticipated this, and wished it. Had Oliver decided otherwise, he would have exerted his influence to have him change his plan.

"Perhaps you are right," said Mr. Kenyon meditatively. "A bright, smart boy like you, is, of course, anxious to get to work and do something for himself. Besides, business men tell me that it is always best to begin young. How old are you?"

"Almost sixteen," answered Oliver.

"I was only fourteen when I commenced business. Yes, I think you are right."

"Is it easy to get a position in the city?" asked Oliver, getting interested.

"Not unless you have influence; but I think I have influence enough to secure you one."

"Thank you, sir."

"In fact, I know of a party who is in want of a boy—an old acquaintance of mine. He will take you to oblige me."

"What business is he in?"

"He has a gentlemen's furnishing store," answered Mr. Kenyon.

"Do you think that business is as good as some other kinds?" said Oliver dubiously.

"It is a capital business," said his step-father emphatically. "Pays splendid profits."

"Who is the gentleman you refer to?" enquired Oliver, with natural interest.

"Well, to be frank with you, it is a nephew of my own. I set him up in business three years ago, and he has paid back every cent of my loan with interest out of the profits of his business. I can assure you it is a paying business."

"I would judge so, from what you say," returned Oliver thoughtfully.

Somehow he felt disappointed to learn that the employer proposed to him should be a relation of his step-father. This, however, was not an objection he could very well express.

"Suppose I should not like business," he suggested, "could I give it up and go to school?"

"Certainly," answered Mr. Kenyon. "Bear in mind, Oliver, that I exercise no compulsion over you. I think you are old enough now to be judge of your own affairs."

"Thank you, sir."

The conversation which we have reported took some time. After it was over Mr. Kenyon devoted his attention to the morning papers, and Oliver was sufficiently amused looking out of the window and examining his fellow-passengers.

Presently they reached the city. Leaving the cars, they got into a horse-car, for distances are great in New York.

Oliver looked out of the car windows with a lively sense of satisfaction. How much gayer and more agreeable it would be, he thought, to be in business in a great city like New York than to live in a quiet little country village where nothing was going on. This was a natural feeling, but there was another side to the question which Oliver did not consider. How many families in the great, gay city are compelled to live in miserable tenements, amid noise and vicious surroundings, who, on the same income, could live comfortably and independently in the country, breathing God's pure air, and with nothing to repel or disgust them ?

"New York is rather a lively place, Oliver," said Mr. Kenyon, who read his young companion's thoughts. "I think you will like to live here."

"I am sure I shall," said Oliver eagerly. "I should think you would prefer it yourself, Mr. Kenyon."

"Perhaps I may remove here some day, Oliver. I own that I have thought of it. Roland would like it better, I am sure."

"Yes, sir, I think he would."

"Where is the store you spoke of, Mr. Kenyon ?" he queried, after a pause. "Are we going there now ?"

"Yes; we will go there in the first place. We may as well get matters settled as soon as possible. Of course, you won't have to go to work immediately. You can take a little time to see the city—say till next Monday."

"Thank, you, sir. I should prefer that."

"We get out here," said Mr. Kenyon after a while.

They were on the Third Avenue line of cars, and it was to a shop on the Bowery that Mr. Kenyon directed his steps. It was by no means a large shop, but the windows were full of articles, labelled with cheap prices, and some even were displayed on the sidewalk. This is a very common practice with shops on the Bowery and Third Avenue, as visitors to New York need not be reminded. On a sign-board over the door the name of the proprietor was conspicuously displayed thus:

EZEKIEL BOND,

Cheap Furnishing Store.

"This is the place, Oliver," said Mr. Kenyon. "Ezekiel Bond is my nephew."

"It seems rather small," commented Oliver, feeling a little disappointed.

"You mustn't judge of the amount of business done by the size of the shop. My nephew's plan is to avoid a large rent, and to replenish his stock frequently. He is a very shrewd and successful man of business. He understands how to manage. The great thing is to make money, Oliver, and Ezekiel knows how to do it. There are many men with large stores, heavy stocks, and great expenses who scarcely make both ends meet. Now, my nephew cleared ten thousand dollars last year. What do you say to that?"

"I shouldn't think it possible to have such a large trade in such a small place," answered Oliver, surprised.

"It is a fact, though. That's a nice income to look forward to, eh, Oliver?"

"Yes, sir."

While this was going on they were standing in front of the window.

"Now," said Mr. Kenyon, "come in and I will introduce you to my nephew."

CHAPTER XIV.

A STORE IN THE BOWERY.

THE store was crowded with a miscellaneous collection of cheap articles. That such a business should yield such large profits struck Oliver with surprise, but he reflected that it was possible, and that he was not qualified to judge of the extent of trade in a city store.

A tall man, pock-marked, and with reddish hair, stood behind the counter, and, with the exception of a young clerk of nineteen, appeared to be the only salesman. This was Ezekiel Bond.

"How are you, Ezekiel?" said Mr. Kenyon affably, advancing to the counter.

"Pretty well, thank you, uncle," said the other, twisting his features into the semblance of a smile. "When did you come into town?"

"This morning only."

"That isn't Roland, is it?"

"Oh, no; it is my step-son, Oliver Conrad. Oliver, this is my nephew, Ezekiel Bond."

"Glad to see you, Mr. Conrad," said Ezekiel, putting out his hand as if he were a pump-handle. "Do you like New York?"

"I haven't seen much of it yet. I think I shall."

"Ezekiel," said Mr. Kenyon, "can I see you a few minutes in private?"

"Oh, certainly. We'll go into the back room. Will Mr. Conrad come, too?"

"No; he can remain with your clerk while we converse."

"John, take care of Mr. Conrad," said Ezekiel.

"All right, sir."

John Meadows was a Bowery boy, and better adapted for the store he was in than for one in a more fashionable thoroughfare.

"The boss wants me to entertain you," he remarked, when they were alone. "How shall I do it?"

"Don't trouble yourself," said Oliver, smiling.

"I'd offer you a cigarette, only the boss don't allow smoking in the store."

"I don't smoke," said Oliver.

"You don't! Where was you brung up?" asked John.

"In the country."

"Oh, that accounts for it. Mean ter say you've never puffed a weed?"

"I never have."

"Then you don't know what 'tis to enjoy yourself. Who's that man you came in with?"

"My step-father."

"I've seen him here before. He's related to my boss. I don't think any more of him for that."

"Why not?" asked Oliver, rather amused. "Don't you like Mr. Bond?"

"Come here," said John.

Oliver approached the counter, and leaning over, John whispered mysteriously:

"He's a file!"

"A what?"

8

"A file, and an awful rasping one at that. He's as mean as dirt."

"I am sorry to hear that, for Mr. Kenyon wants me to begin business in this store."

John whistled.

"That's a go," he said. "Are you going to do it?"

"I suppose I shall try it. If I don't like it I can give it up at any time."

"Then I wish I was you. I don't like it, but I can't give it up, or I might have to live on nothing a week. I don't see what the boss wants an extra hand for. There aint enough trade to keep us busy."

"Mr. Kenyon tells me Mr. Bond has made money."

"Well, I am glad to hear it. The boss is always a-complainin' that trade is dull, and he must cut me down. If he does I'll sink into a hungry grave, that's all."

"How much do you get!" asked Oliver, amused by his companion's tone.

"Eight dollars a week; and what's that to support a gentleman on? I tell you what, I haven't had a new necktie for three months."

"That is hard."

"Hard! I should say it was hard. Look at them shoes!"

And John, bounding over the counter, displayed a foot which had successfully struggled out of its encasement on one side. "Isn't it disgraceful that a gentleman should have to wear such foot-cases as them?"

"Won't Mr. Bond pay you more?" asked Oliver.

"I guess not. I asked him last week, and he lectured me on the dulness of trade. Then he went on for to show that eight dollars was a fortune, and I'd orter keep my carriage on it. He's a regular old file, he is."

"From what you say, I don't think I shall get very high pay," said Oliver.

"It's different with you. You're a relation. You'll be took care of."

"I'm not related to Mr. Bond," said Oliver, sensible of a feeling of repugnance. "If it depends on that, I shall expect no favors."

"You'll get 'em, all the same. His uncle's your step-father."

"Where do you live?"

"Oh, I've got a room round on Bleecker Street. It's about big enough for a good-sized cat to live in. I have to double myself up nights so as not to overflow into the entry."

"Why don't you get a better room?"

"Why don't I live on Fifth Avenue, and set up my carriage? 'Cause it can't be done on eight dollars a week. I have to live accordin' to my income."

"That's where you are right. How much do you have to pay for your room?"

"A dollar and a half a week."

"I don't ask from curiosity. I suppose I shall have to get a place somewhere."

"When you get ready, come to me. I'll find you a place."

Here an old lady entered—an old lady from the country evidently, in a bombazine dress and a bonnet which might have been in fashion twenty years before. She was short-sighted, and peered inquisitively at Oliver and John.

"Which of you youngsters keeps this store?" she enquired.

"I am the gentleman, ma'am," said John, with a flourish.

"Oh, you be! Well, I'm from the country."

"Never should have thought it, ma'am. You look like an uptown lady I know—Mrs. General Buster."

"You don't say," returned the old lady, evidently feeling complimented. "I'm Mrs. Deacon Grimes of Pottsville."

"Is the deacon well?" asked John, with a ludicrous assumption of interest.

"He's pooty smart," answered Mrs. Grimes, "though he's troubled sometimes with a pain in the back."

"So am I," said John; "but I know what to do for it."

"What do you do?"

"Have somebody rub me down with a brick-bat."

"The deacon wouldn't allow no one to do that," said the old lady, accepting the remedy in good faith.

"Can I sell you a silk necktie this morning, ma'am?" asked John.

"No; I want some handkerchers for the deacon; red silk ones he wants."

"We haven't any of that kind. Here's some nice cotton ones, a good deal cheaper."

"Will they wash?" asked Mrs. Grimes cautiously.

"Of course they will. We import 'em ourselves."

"Well, I don't know. If you'll sell 'em real cheap I'll take two."

Then ensued a discussion of the price, which Oliver found very amusing. Finally the old lady took two handkerchiefs and retired.

"Is that the way you do business?" asked Oliver.

"Yes. We have all sorts of customers, and have to please 'em all. The old woman wanted to know if they would wash. The color 'll all wash out in one washing."

"I am afraid you cheated her, then."

"What's the odds? She wasn't willing to pay for a good article."

"I don't believe I can do business that way," thought Oliver.

Just then Mr. Kenyon returned with Ezekiel Bond from the back room in which they had been conferring.

"It's all settled, Oliver," he said. "Mr. Bond has agreed to take you, and you are to begin work next Monday morning."

Oliver bowed. The place did not seem quite so desirable to him now.

"I will be on hand," he answered.

When Mr. Kenyon and he had left the store, the former said :

"Every Saturday evening Mr. Bond will hand you twelve dollars, out of which you will be expected to defray all your expenses."

"The other clerk told me he only got eight."

"Part of this sum comes from me. I don't want you to be pinched. You have been brought up differently from him. I hope you'll like my nephew."

"I hope I shall," said Oliver, but his tone implied doubt.

CHAPTER XV.

OLIVER didn't go back to his native village. Mr. Kenyon sent on his trunk, and thus obviated the necessity. Our hero took up his quarters at a cheap hotel until, with the help of John Meadows, he obtained a room in St. Mark's Place. The room was a large square one, tolerably well furnished. The price asked was four dollars a week.

"That is rather more than I ought to pay just for a room," said Oliver.

"I'll tell you how you can get it cheaper," said John Meadows.

"How?"

"Take me for your room-mate. I'll pay a dollar and a half toward the rent."

Oliver hesitated, but finally decided to accept John's offer. Though his fellow-clerk was not altogether to his taste, it would pre-

vent his feeling lonely, and he had no other
acquaintances to select from.

"All right," he said.

"Is it a bargain?" said John, delighted.
"I'll give my Bleecker Street landlady notice
right off. Why, I shall feel like a prince
here!"

"Then this is better than your room?"

"You bet! That's only big enough for a
middling sized cat, while this——"

"Is big enough for two large ones," said
Oliver, smiling.

"Yes, and a whole litter of kittens into the
bargain. We'll have a jolly time together."

"I hope so."

"Of course," said John seriously, "when
I get married that 'll terminate the con-
tract."

"Do you think of getting married soon?"
asked Oliver, surprised and amused.

"I'll tell you about it," said John, with the
utmost gravity. "Last month I had my
fortune told."

"Well?"

"It was told by Mme. Catalina, the seventh

daughter of a seventh daughter; so, of course, she wasn't a humbug."

"Does that make any difference—being the seventh daughter?"

"Of course it does. Well, she told me that I should marry a rich widow, and ever after live in luxury," said John, evidently elated by his prospects.

"Did you believe her?"

"Of course I did. She told things that I knew to be true about the past, and that convinced me she could foretell the future."

"Such as what?"

"She told me I had lately had a letter from a person who was interested in me. So I had. I got a letter from Charlie Cameron only a week before. Me and Charlie went to school together, so, of course, he feels interested in me."

"What else?"

"She said a girl with black eyes was in love with me."

"Is that true?"

John nodded complacently.

"Who is it?"

"I don't know her name, but I've met her two or three times on the street, and she always looked at me and smiled."

"Struck with your looks, I suppose," suggested Oliver.

John stroked an incipient mustache and stole a look into the glass.

"Looks like it," he said.

"If she were only a rich widow you wouldn't mind cultivating her acquaintance ?"

"I wish she were," said John thoughtfully.

"You haven't any widow in view, have you ?"

"Yes, I have," said John, rather to Oliver's surprise.

"Who is it ?"

"Her husband used to keep a lager-beer saloon on Bleecker Street, and now the widow carries it on. I've enquired about, and I hear she's worth ten thousand dollars. Would you like to see her ?"

"Very much," answered Oliver, whose curiosity was excited.

"Come along, then. We'll drop in and get a couple of glasses of something."

Following his guide, or rather side by side, Oliver walked round to the saloon.

"Does she know you admire her?" enquired Oliver.

"I don't," said John. "I admire her money."

"Would you be willing to sell yourself?"

"For ten thousand dollars? I guess I would. That's the easiest way of getting rich. It would take me two hundred years, at eight dollars a week, to make such a fortune."

They entered the saloon. Behind the counter stood a woman of thirty-five, weighing upward of two hundred pounds. She looked good-natured, but the idea of a marriage between her and John Meadows, a youth of nineteen, seemed too ridiculous.

"What will you have?" she asked, in a Teutonic accent.

"Sarsaparilla and lager!" answered John.

Frau Winterhammer filled two mugs in the most business-like manner. She evidently had no idea that John was an admirer.

In the same business-like manner she received the money he laid on the counter.

John smacked his lips in affected delight.

"It is very good," he said.   "Your lager is always good, Mrs. Winterhammer."

"So !" replied the good woman.

"That's so !" repeated John.

"Then perhaps you comes again," said the frau, with an eye to business.

"Oh, yes ; I'll be sure to come again," said John, with a tender significance which was quite lost upon the matter-of-fact lady.

"And you bring your friends, too," she suggested.

"Yes ; I will bring my friends."

"Dat is good," said Mrs. Winterhammer, in a satisfied tone.

Having no excuse for stopping longer the two friends went out.

"What do you think of her, Oliver ?" asked John.

"There's a good deal of her," answered Oliver, using a non-committal phrase.

"Yes, she's rather plump," said John.   "I don't like a skeleton, for my part."

"She doesn't look much like one."

"She's good-looking; don't you think so?" enquired John, looking anxiously in his companion's face.

"She looks pleasant; but, John, she's a good deal older than you."

"She's about thirty."

"Nearer forty."

"Oh, no, she isn't. And she's worth ten thousand dollars! Think, Oliver, how nice it would be to be worth ten thousand dollars! I wouldn't clerk it for old Bond any more, I can tell you that."

"Would you keep the saloon?"

"No, I'd let her keep that and I'd set up in something else. We'd double the money in a short time and then I'd retire and go to Europe."

"That's all very well, John; but suppose she won't have you?"

John smiled—a self-satisfied smile.

"She wouldn't reject a stylish young fellow like me—do you think she would? She'd feel flattered to get such a young husband."

"Perhaps she would," said Oliver, who thought John under a strange hallucination.

"You must invite me to the wedding whenever it comes off, John."

"You shall be my groomsman," answered John confidently.

A week later John said to Oliver after supper:

"Oliver, I'm goin' to do it."

"To do what?"

"I'm goin' to propose to the widder to-night."

"So soon!"

"Yes; I'm tired of workin' for old Bond; I want to go in for myself."

"Well, John, I wish you good luck, but I shall be sorry to lose you for a room-mate."

"Lend me a necktie, won't you, Oliver? I want to take her eye, you know."

So Oliver lent his most showy necktie to his room-mate, and John departed on his important mission.

About half an hour later John rushed into the room in a violent state of excitement, his collar and bosom looking as if they had been soaked in dirty water, and sank into a chair.

"What's the matter?" asked Oliver.

"I've cast her off!" answered John in a hollow voice. "She is a faithless deceiver."

"Tell me all about it, Jack."

John told his story. He went to the saloon, ordered a glass of lager, and after drinking it asked the momentous question. Frau Winter-hammer seemed surprised, said "So!" and then called "Fritz!" A stout fellow in shirt-sleeves came out of a rear room, and the widow said something to him in German. Then he seized John's arms, and the widow deliberately threw the contents of a pitcher of lager in his face and bosom. Then both laughed rudely, and John was released.

"What shall you do about it, John?" asked Oliver, with difficulty refraining from laughing.

"I have cast her off!" he said gloomily, "I will never enter the saloon again."

"I wouldn't," said Oliver.

Oliver would have felt less like laughing had he known that at that very moment Ezekiel Bond, prompted by Mr. Kenyon, was conspiring to get him into trouble.

CHAPTER XVI.

THE CONSPIRACY.

OLIVER did not find his work in the store very laborious. During some parts of the day there was little custom, and therefore little to do. At such times he found John Meadows, though not a refined, at any rate an amusing companion. With his friendly help he soon got a general idea of the stock and the prices. He found that the former was generally of an inferior quality, and the customers belonged to the poorer classes. Obtaining a general idea of the receipts, he began to doubt Mr. Kenyon's assurance of the profits of the business. He intimated as much to his fellow-clerk.

"The old man sold you," he said. "Bond doesn't take in more than twenty thousand dollars a year, and there isn't more than a tenth profit."

"You are sure of that, John?"

"Yes."

"Then Mr. Kenyon has deceived me. I wonder what for."

"Does he love you very much?"

"Who?"

"Old Kenyon."

"Not enough to hurt him," said Oliver, with a smile.

"Then he wanted to get rid of you, and made you think this was a splendid opening."

"I don't know but you are right," returned Oliver thoughtfully. "He seemed very kind, though."

"He's an old fox. I knew it as soon as I set eyes on him."

"I didn't enjoy myself much at home. I would just as soon be here. I don't like this store particularly, but I like New York."

"Lots goin' on here all the time. Don't you want to go out in a torchlight procession to-night? I can get you the chance."

"No, I think not."

"I like it. I've been out ever so many times. Sometimes I'm a Democrat and some-

times I'm a Republican. It makes no difference to me so long as I have fun."

Three weeks passed without developing anything to affect our hero's fortunes.

About this time Ezekiel Bond received the
following note from his uncle:

I think you may as well carry out, without any further delay, the plan on which you agreed when Oliver
entered your employment. I consider it desirable that
he should be got rid of at once. As soon as anything
happens, apprise me by letter.

B. KENYON.

Ezekiel Bond shrugged his shoulders when
he received this letter.

"I can't quite understand what Uncle Benjamin is driving at," he said to himself.
"He's got the property, and I can't see how
the boy stands in the way. However, I am
under obligations to him, and must carry out
his wishes."

Ten minutes later he entered the store from
the back room, and said to Oliver:

"Have you any objection to going out for
me?"

"No, sir," answered Oliver with alacrity.

He was glad to escape for a time from the confinement of the store and breathe the outside air.   John Meadows would have rebelled against being employed as an errand boy, but Oliver had no such pride.

"Here is a sealed letter which I wish carried to the address marked on it.   Be careful of it for it contains a twenty-dollar bill. Look out for pick-pockets."

"Yes, sir."

Oliver put the letter in his coat pocket, put on his hat, and went out into the street.   The distance was about a mile, but as trade was dull at that hour, he decided to walk, knowing that he could easily be spared from the store.

The note was addressed to a tailor who had been making a business coat for Mr. Bond.

Oliver entered the tailor's shop and inquired for James Norcross, the head of the establishment.

An elderly man said : "That is my name," and opened the letter.

He read it, and then turned to Oliver.

"Where is the money ! " he demanded.

"What money?" asked Oliver, surprised.

"Your employer writes me that he encloses twenty dollars—the amount due me—and wishes me to send back a receipt by you."

"Well, sir?"

"There is no money in the letter," said the tailor, looking sharply at Oliver.

"I don't understand it at all, sir," said Oliver, disturbed.

"Has the letter gone out of your possession?"

"No, sir. I put it in my pocket and it has remained there."

"How, then, could the money be lost?"

"I think Mr. Bond may have neglected to put it in. Shall I go back and ask him about it?"

Again Mr. Norcross looked in Oliver's face. Certainly there was no guilt expressed there, only concerned surprise.

"Perhaps you had better," he said. "You saw me open the letter?"

"Yes, sir."

"Then you can bear witness that there was nothing in it. Report this to Mr. Bond, and ask him to send me up the money to-morrow at latest, as I need it to help meet a note."

"I will, sir. I am sorry there has been any mistake about it."

"Mr. Bond must certainly have forgotten to put in the bill. I presume he has found out his mistake by this time," thought Oliver.

He had no suspicion that there was no mistake at all—that it was a conspiracy against his own reputation, instigated by Mr. Kenyon, and artfully carried out by Ezekiel Bond.

CHAPTER XVII.

OLIVER LOSES HIS PLACE.

OLIVER re-entered the store and went up to Mr. Bond, who was standing behind the counter awaiting his return.

"Have you brought back the receipt?" asked his employer, before he had a chance to speak.

"No, sir."

"Why not?" demanded Bond, frowning.

"There was some mistake, Mr. Bond. The letter you gave me contained no money."

"Contained no money! What do you mean?" exclaimed the storekeeper.

Oliver briefly related the circumstances, repeating that the letter contained no money.

"Do you mean to tell me such an unblushing falsehood," demanded Ezekiel Bond, "expecting me to believe it?"

"Mr. Bond," said Oliver, with dignity, "it

is just as I say. There was no money in the letter."

"Silence!" roared Bond, working himself up into a premeditated excitement. "I tell you I put the money in myself. I think I ought to know whether there was any money in it."

"It is very strange, sir. I saw Mr. Norcross open the letter. If he had taken any bill out, I should have seen it."

"I presume you would," sneered Bond. "I dare say he did find the letter empty."

Oliver looked puzzled. He was not yet prepared for an accusation. He attributed Mr. Bond's anger to his annoyance at the loss of twenty dollars. He kept silent, but waited to hear what else his employer had to say.

"I can understand this strange matter," continued Ezekiel, with another sneer. "I am not altogether a fool, and I can tell you why no bill was found."

"Why, sir?"

"Because you opened the letter and took the money out before you reached the tailor's."

He was about to say more, but Oliver interrupted him by an indignant denial.

"That's a lie, sir!" he said hotly. "I don't care who says it."

"Do you mean to tell me I lie?" exclaimed Ezekiel Bond, purple with rage.

"If you charge me with stealing the money, I do!" said Oliver, his face flaming with just indignation.

"You hear that, John Meadows?" said Ezekiel, turning to his other clerk. "Did you ever hear such impudence?"

John Meadows was not a coward nor a sneak, and he had not the slightest belief in Oliver's guilt. To his credit, he dared manfully to avow it.

"Mr. Bond," he answered, "I don't believe Oliver would do such a thing. I know him well, and I've always found him right side up with care."

"Thank you, John," said Oliver gratefully. "I am glad there is one who believes I am not a thief."

"You don't believe he is guilty because you are honest yourself, John," said Mr. Bond, willing to gain over his older clerk by a little flattery. "But how can it be otherwise? I put the money very carefully in the envelope. Oliver put it in his pocket, and when he hands the letter to Mr. Norcross it is empty."

"Are you sure you put the money in, sir?" asked John.

"Am I sure the sun rose this morning?" retorted Mr. Bond. "Of course, I am certain; and I am morally certain that Oliver took the money. Hark, you! I will give you one chance to redeem yourself," he continued, addressing our hero. "Give me back the money and I will forgive you this time."

"Mr. Bond," said Oliver indignantly, "you insult me by speaking in that way! Once for all, I tell you that I don't know anything about the money, and no one who knows me will believe your charge. You may search me if you want to."

"It would do no great good," said Bond sarcastically. "You have had plenty of chances to dispose of the money. You could easily pass it over to some confederate."

"Mr. Bond," said Oliver, "I see that you

are determined to have people believe me guilty. I think I understand what it all means. It is a conspiracy to destroy my reputation. You know there was no money in the letter you sent by me."

"Say that again, you young rascal, and I will give you a flogging!" shouted Ezekiel Bond, now really angry, for he was conscious that Oliver spoke the truth, and the truth is very distasteful sometimes.

"I don't think you will," retorted our hero undauntedly; "there are policemen in the city, and I should give you in charge."

"You would, would you? I have a great mind to have you arrested for theft."

"Do, if you like. I am willing to have the matter investigated."

It was evident that in attempting to frighten Oliver Mr. Bond had undertaken a difficult job. He would really have liked to give Oliver in charge, but he knew very well that he could prove nothing against him. Besides, he would be exceeding the instructions which Mr. Kenyon had given him, and this he did not venture to do. There was, however, one way of revenge open to him, and this was in strict accordance with his orders.

"I will spare you the disgrace of arrest," he said, "not for your own sake, but for the sake of my esteemed uncle, who will be deeply grieved when he hears of this occurrence. But I cannot consent any longer to retain you in my employment. I will not ask my faithful clerk, John Meadows, to associate with a thief."

"I don't care to remain in your employment, Mr. Bond. I would not consent to, until you retracted your false charge. As to you, John," he continued, turning to John Meadows, with a smile, "I hope you are not afraid to associate with me."

"I guess 'twon't hurt me much," said John courageously. "I think Mr. Bond has made a great mistake in suspecting you."

"You judge him by yourself," said Mr. Bond, who chose not to fall out with John. "You may do as you please, but I can no longer employ a suspicious character."

"Good-morning, Mr. Bond," said Oliver proudly. "I will lose no time in relieving you of my presence. John, I will see you to-night."

"One word more," said his employer. "I shall deem it my duty to acquaint my uncle with my reasons for dismissing you. I know it will grieve him deeply."

"I think he will manage to live through it," said Oliver sarcastically. "I shall also send him an account of the occurrence, and he may believe whichever of us he pleases."

Oliver took his hat and left the store.

"I fear he is a hardened young rascal, John," Bond remarked to his remaining clerk, with a hypocritical sigh. "My uncle warned me that I might have trouble with him, when he first placed him here."

"I never saw anything bad in him, Mr. Bond," said John. "I am sorry he is gone."

"He has deceived you, and I am not surprised. He is very artful—exceedingly artful!" repeated Ezekiel, emphasizing the adverb by prolonging its pronunciation. "I don't mind the loss of the money so much as I do losing my confidence in him. So young, and such a reprobate! It is sad—sad!"

"He does it well," thought John. "What a precious old file he is, to be sure! I don't believe old Kenyon is any better, either. They come of the same stock, and it's a bad one."

Before the store closed for the day, Ezekiel said:

"Shall you see Oliver to-night?"

"I expect to, sir."

"Then I will trouble you to give him this money—six dollars. I owe him for half a week, and it was at that rate my uncle requested me to pay him. Twelve dollars a week! Why, he might have grown rich on that, if he had remained honest."

"I wish you would give me the same chance, Mr. Bond," said John. "I can't rub along very well on eight."

"Don't ask me now, just after I have been robbed of twenty dollars. I can't afford it."

"I wish I could get another place," thought John. "I should like to work for a man I could respect, even if he didn't pay me any more."

CHAPTER XVIII.

OLIVER, THE OUTCAST.

WITHOUT much hope of obtaining sympathy or credence, Oliver wrote to his step-father an account of the charge which Mr. Bond had brought against him, and denied in the most positive terms its truth.

"There," he said to himself as he posted the letter, "that is all I can do. Mr. Kenyon must now decide which he will believe."

Until he should hear from his step-father he decided not to form any plans for the future. One thing he was decided upon, not to return home. Since his mother's death (for he supposed her dead) it was no home for him. He had been in the city long enough to become fond of city life, and he meant to remain there. If Mr. Kenyon chose to assist him to procure another situation, he would accept his proffered aid, otherwise he would try to earn his own living.

Two days later he received a letter, which he at once perceived to be in his step-father's handwriting. He tore it open eagerly and began to read. His lip curled with scorn before he had read far.

These were the material portions of the letter:

The same mail brought me letters from you and Mr. Bond. I need not say how grieved I am to hear that you have subjected yourself to a criminal charge. The circumstances leave no doubt of your guilt. Unhappy boy! how, with the liberal allowance you received, could you stoop to so mean, so dishonorable a theft? My nephew writes me that with brazen effrontery you denied your guilt, though it was self-evident, and treated his remonstrances with the most outrageous insolence. It is well, indeed, that your poor mother did not live to see this day.

"How dare he refer to my mother!" exclaimed Oliver indignantly, when he came to this passage.

He went on with the letter:

I didn't expect that my well-meant and earnest effort to start you on a business career would terminate in this way. I confess I am puzzled to know what to do with you. I cannot take you home, for I do not wish Roland corrupted by your example.

Here Oliver's lip curled again with scorn.

Nor can I recommend you to another place. Knowing you to be dishonest, I should feel that I was doing wrong to give you a good character. I will not tell your old acquaintances here of your sad wickedness. I have too much consideration for you. I have only told Roland, hoping that it may be a warning to him, though I am thankful that he at least is incapable of theft.

After anxious consideration, I have decided that you have forfeited all claim to any further help from me. I cast you off, and shall leave you henceforth to shift for yourself. You cannot justly complain, for you must be sensible that you have brought this upon yourself. I intended, sooner or later, to buy an interest for you in my nephew's business,—that is, if you behaved properly, —but all this is at an end now. I enclose twenty dollars to help you along until you can get something to do. I advise you to enlist on some ship as cabin-boy. There you will be out of reach of temptation, and may, in time, lead a useful, though humble career.

I need not say with how much grief I write these words. It pains me to cast you off, but I cannot own any connection with a thief. Roland is also grieved by the news. Hoping that you may live to see the error of your ways, I subscribe myself,

BENJAMIN KENYON.

Oliver read this letter with indignation and amazement.

Was it possible that Mr. Kenyon, while in

10

the possession of a large property left him by his mother, could thus coolly cast him off, and leave him to support himself?

He wrote the following reply:

MR. KENYON:

I have received your harsh and unjust letter. I am innocent, and you know it. Of the large property which my mother left, you send me twenty dollars, and keep the remainder. I shall keep and use the money, for it is justly mine. Sometime you will repent de-frauding an orphan. I don't think I shall starve, but I shall not soon forget your treachery. Some day—I don't know when—I will punish you for it.

OLIVER CONRAD.

CHAPTER XIX.

A STRANGE ACQUAINTANCE.

MR. KENYON shrugged his shoulders, and smiled, when he read Oliver's letter.

"So the young cub is showing his claws, is he?" he said to himself. "I fancy he will find it harder to punish me than he supposes. Where will he get the power? Money is power, and I have the money. Yes," he continued, his sallow face lighting up with exultation, "I have played boldly for it, and it is mine! Who shall dispute my claim? My wife is in a mad-house, and likely to remain there, and now Oliver is disposed of. I wish he would go to sea, and never be heard of again. But at any rate I am pretty safe so far as he is concerned."

Oliver did not expect to terrify Mr. Kenyon with his threats. He, too, felt his present want of power; but he was young, and he could wait. Indeed, the question of punishing his step-father was not the one that first demanded his attention. He had but twenty dollars in the world, and no expectations. He must find work of some kind, and that soon. Now, unluckily for Oliver, the times were hard. There were thousands out of employment, and fifty applications where there was one vacancy. Day after day he answered advertisements without effect. Only once he had a favorable answer. This was in a great dry-goods house.

"Yes," said the superintendent, who was pleased with his appearance and manners, "we will take you, if you like to come."

Oliver brightened up. His sky seemed to be clearing.

"Perhaps you will object to the pay we give," said the superintendent.

"I don't expect much," said our hero, who thought he would accept for the present, if he were only offered six dollars.

"We will pay you two dollars a week for the first six months."

"Two dollars a week!" exclaimed Oliver in dismay.

"For the first six months. Then we will raise you to four if you do well."

"Then I can't come," said Oliver despondently. "I shall have to live on my salary, and I couldn't possibly live on two dollars a week."

"I am sorry," said the superintendent; "but as we can get plenty of boys for two dollars, we cannot break our rule."

Oliver went out, rather indignant.

"No wonder boys are tempted to steal," he thought, "when employers are so mean."

It was getting rather serious for him. His money had been dwindling daily.

"John," he said to his room-mate one evening, "I must give up this room at the end of the week."

"Are you out of funds?"

"I have but fifty cents left in the world."

"I can't keep the room alone. When is our week up?"

"To-morrow evening."

"I will take my old room. I know it is still vacant. What will you do?"

"I don't know. I haven't money enough to take any room."

"I wish I had some money to lend you; I'd do it in a minute," said John heartily.

"I know you would, John, but you have hard work scraping along yourself."

"I'll tell you what I can do. Come to my little room, and we'll take turns sleeping in the bed. It is only eighteen inches wide, or we could both occupy it at a time."

"I'll come round and sleep on the floor, John. I won't deprive you of your bed. I wish I knew what to do."

"Perhaps Mr. Bond would take you back."

"No, he wouldn't. I am convinced that there was a conspiracy to get rid of me. I might try my hand at selling papers."

"You are too much of a gentleman to go into the street with the ragged street boys."

"My gentility won't supply me with board and lodging. I mustn't think of that."

"Something may turn up for you to-morrow, Oliver."

"It won't do to depend on that. If I can

turn up something, that will be more to the purpose. However, this is our last night in this room, and I won't worry myself into a sleepless night. I will get my money's worth out of the bed."

Oliver was not given to dismal forebodings or to anticipating trouble, though he certainly might have been excused for feeling depressed under present circumstances. He slept soundly, and went out in the morning, active and alert.

He took a cheap breakfast—a cup of coffee and some tea-biscuit—for ten cents. He rose from the table with an appetite, but he didn't dare to spend more money. As it was, he had but forty cents left.

About one o'clock, after applying at several stores for employment, but ineffectually, he found himself standing at the corner of Fifth Avenue and Fourteenth Street.

A tall gentleman, with a dignified air, probably seventy years of age, accosted him as he stood there.

"My young friend," he said, "will you dine with me?"

Oliver looked at him in astonishment to see if he was in earnest.

"I do not wish to dine alone," said the other. "Be my guest unless you have dined."

"No, sir, I have not dined; but I am a stranger to you."

"Very true; we shall get acquainted before dinner is over."

"Then I will accept your invitation with pleasure, sir. It is the more acceptable because I am out of a situation and have very little money."

"You are well dressed."

"Very true, sir. My dress is deceptive, however."

"All that is irrelevant. Come, if you please."

So Oliver followed his new acquaintance to Delmonico's restaurant. They selected a small table, and a waiter approached to receive orders.

"I hope you are hungry," said the old gentleman. "Pray do justice to my invitation."

Oliver smiled.

"I can easily do that, sir," he said. "I made but a light breakfast."

"So much the better. What kind of soup will you have?"

Oliver selected turtle soup, which was speedily brought.

It is unnecessary to enter into an elaborate description of the dinner. It is enough that Oliver redeemed his promise, and ate heartily; his new acquaintance regarding him with approval.

"Will you have some wine?" he asked.

"No, sir," replied Oliver.

"You had better try some champagne."

"No, thank you."

"At least you will take some coffee?"

"Thank you, sir."

The coffee was brought, and at length the dinner was over.

"Thank you, sir," said Oliver, preparing to leave his hospitable entertainer. "You have been very kind. I will bid you good-day."

"No, no, come home with me. I want to have a talk with you."

Oliver reflected that his new acquaintance,

who had been so mysteriously kind, might be disposed to furnish him with some employment, and thought it best to accept the invitation, especially as his time was of little value.

Twenty minutes' walk brought them to the door of a fine brown-stone house on a street leading out of Fifth Avenue.

The old gentleman took out a latch-key, opened the front door, and signed to Oliver to follow him upstairs. He paused before a front room on the third floor. Both entered. The room was in part an ordinary bed-chamber, but not wholly. In one corner was a rosewood case containing a number of steel instruments.

The old gentleman's face lighted up with strange triumph, and he locked the door.

Oliver thought it singular, but suspected no harm.

"Now, my young friend," said the old man, "I will tell you why I brought you here."

"If you please, sir."

"I am a physician, and am in search of a hidden principle of nature, which I am satisfied can only be arrived at by vivisection."

"By what, sir?" exclaimed Oliver, whom the feverish, excited air of the old man began to startle.

"I propose to cut you up," said the old man composedly, selecting an ugly looking instrument, "and watch carefully the——"

"Are you mad, sir?" exclaimed Oliver, aghast. "Do you wish to murder me?"

"You will die in behalf of science," said the old doctor calmly. "Your death, through my observations, will be a blessing to the race. Be good enough to take off your coat."

Oliver was horror-struck. The door was locked, and the old man stood between him and escape. It was evident that he was in the power of a maniac.

"Is my life to end thus?" he asked himself, in affright.

CHAPTER XX.

A TERRIBLE SITUATION.

"BE good enough to remove your coat," said the old man with a politeness hardly consistent with his fearful purpose.

"Sir," said Oliver, hoping that he might be accessible to reason, "you have no right to experiment upon me without my permission."

"I should prefer your permission," said the old doctor.

"I can't give it," said Oliver hastily.

"My young friend," said the old man, with an air of superior wisdom, "you do not appreciate the important part you are invited to take in the progress of scientific discovery. You will lose your life, to be sure, but what is a single life to the discovery of a great truth! Your name will live for ages in connection with the great principle which I shall have the honor of discovering."

"I would rather live myself," said Oliver

bluntly. "Science may be all very well, but I prefer that somebody else should have the privilege of dying to promote it."

"They all say so," said the old man musingly. "No one has the noble courage to sacrifice himself for the truth."

"I shouldn't think they would," retorted Oliver. "Why don't you experiment on yourself?"

"I would willingly, but there are two impediments. I cannot at once be operator and subject. Besides, I am too old. My natural force is abated, while you are young, strong, and vigorous. Oh, yes," and he looked gloatingly at our hero, "you will be a capital subject."

"Look here," said Oliver desperately, "I tell you I won't be a subject."

"Then I must proceed without your permission," said the old doctor calmly. "I have already waited too long. I cannot let this opportunity slip."

"If you kill me you will be hanged!" exclaimed Oliver, the perspiration starting from every pore.

"I will submit cheerfully to an ignominious

death, if time is only given me to complete and announce my discovery," said the old man composedly.

Evidently he was in earnest. Poor Oliver did not know what to do. He determined, however, to keep the old man in conversation as long as possible, hoping that help might yet arrive, and the struggle—for he meant to fight for his life—be avoided.

"Did you have this in view when you invited me to dine with you?" he asked.

"Surely I did."

"Why did you select me rather than some-one else?"

"Because you are so young and vigorous. You are in the full flush of health."

Now this is a very pleasant assurance in ordinary cases, but under the circumstances Oliver did not enjoy the compliment. A thought struck him.

"You are mistaken," he said. "I am not as well as I look. I have—heart disease."

"I can hardly believe it," said the old man. "Heart disease does not go with such a physique."

" I've got it," said Oliver. " If you want a perfectly healthy subject, you must apply to someone else."

" I will test it," said the old man, approaching. " If you really are subject to disease of the heart, you will not answer my purpose."

" Put down that knife, then," said Oliver.

The doctor put it down. Oliver shuddered while the relentless devotee of science placed his hand over his heart, and waited anxiously his decision.

It came.

" You are mistaken, my young friend," he said. " The movement of your heart is slightly accelerated, but it is in a perfectly healthy state."

" I don't believe you can tell," said Oliver desperately, " just by holding your hand over it a minute."

" Science is unerring, my young friend," said the old man calmly. " But we waste time. Take off your coat and prepare yourself for the operation."

The crisis had come, the old man approached with his dangerous weapon. At this supreme moment Oliver espied a bell-knob. He sprang to it, and rang a peal that echoed through the house, and was distinctly heard even in the chamber where they were standing.

"What did you do that for?" demanded the old man angrily.

"I am not going to stay here to be murdered!" exclaimed Oliver. "I give you warning that I will resist you with all my strength."

"You would foil me, would you?" exclaimed the maniac, now thoroughly excited. "It must not be "

Oliver hurriedly put a chair between himself and the old man.

At that moment steps were heard on the staircase, and someone tried the door.

"Help!" shouted Oliver, encouraged by what he heard.

"What is the matter?" demanded a voice outside. "Father, what are you doing?"

The old man looked disgusted and mortified.

"Go away!" he said querulously.

"Who is there with you?"

"No one."

"It's a lie!" said Oliver, in a loud voice. "I am a boy who has been lured in here by this old man, who wants to murder me."

"Open the door at once, father," said the voice outside sternly.

The old man was apparently overawed and afraid to refuse. He advanced sullenly and turned the key. The door was at once opened from outside.

A man in middle life entered. He took in the situation at a glance.

"You are at your tricks again, sir," he said sternly to the old man. "Put down that knife."

The old man obeyed.

"Don't be harsh, Samuel," he said, in an apologetic tone. "You know that I am working in the interests of science."

"Don't try to impose on me with such nonsense. What were you going to do with that boy?"

"I wished to experiment upon him."

"You were going to murder him, and the

11

law would have exacted the penalty had I not interfered."

"I would have submitted, if I could have only demonstrated the great principle which——"

"The great humbug! Promise me that you will never again attempt any such folly, or I shall be compelled to send you back to the hospital."

"Don't send me there, Samuel!" said the old man, shuddering.

"Then take care you do not make it necessary. Young man, come with me."

It may be imagined that Oliver gladly accepted the invitation.

He followed his guide downstairs, and into the parlor, which was very handsomely furnished.

"What is your name?" enquired the other.

"Oliver Conrad."

"How came you with my father?"

Oliver told the story briefly.

"I am very much mortified at the imposition that has been practised upon you, and alarmed at the thought of what might have happened but for my accidental presence at home. Of course you can see for yourself that my father is insane."

"Yes, sir, I can see it now; but I did not suspect it when we first met."

"I suppose not. In fact, he is not generally insane. He is rather a monomaniac."

"It seems a dangerous kind of monomania."

"You are right; it is. Unless I can control him at home, I must send him back to the hospital. He has been an eminent physician, and until two years ago was in active practice. His delusion is connected with his profession, and is therefore less likely to be cured. I am surprised that you accepted a stranger's invitation to dine."

"I will tell you frankly, sir," said Oliver, "that I am out of employment, and have but forty cents in the world. You could hardly expect me to decline a dinner at Delmonico's under the circumstances."

"To be sure," said the other thoughtfully. "Wait here one minute, please."

He left the room, but returned in less than

five minutes. He handed a sealed envelope to Oliver.

" I owe you some reparation for the danger to which you have been exposed. Accept the enclosure, and do me the favor not to mention the events of to-day."

Oliver thanked him and made the promise requested.

When he was in the street he opened the envelope. To his amazement, it proved to contain one hundred dollars in bills!

"Shall I take this!" he asked himself.

Necessity answered for him.

" It is a strange way of earning money," he thought. "I shouldn't like to go through it again. On the whole, however, this is a lucky day. I have had a dinner at Delmonico's, and I have money enough to last me ten weeks at least."

CHAPTER XXI.

ROLAND IS SURPRISED.

OLIVER was walking along Broadway in very good spirits, as he well might, after such an extraordinary piece of good fortune, when all at once he became sensible that his step-brother, Roland, was approaching him.

His first impulse was to avoid the meeting by crossing the street; but, after all, why should he avoid Roland? He had done nothing to be ashamed of. Certainly, Roland was not his friend, but he had been his companion so long that there was something homelike in his face.

Roland recognized him at the instant of meeting.

"Oliver!" he exclaimed in surprise.

"How are you, Roland?" said Oliver composedly.

Roland colored and looked embarrassed.

" Are you still in the city ? " he asked.

" You see I am."

" My father told me you were going to sea."

" He advised me to go to sea, but I have not followed his advice."

"I should think you would."

" Why should you think I would ? Do you think of going to sea ? "

"Of course not."

"Then why should I ? "

" It must be rather awkward for you to stay in New York. Are you not afraid of being arrested ? "

"Arrested ! " repeated Oliver haughtily. "What do you mean ? "

" You know well enough what I mean. On account of the money you stole from my cousin."

"Say that again and I will knock you over ! "

" You wouldn't dare to—in the public street ! " said Roland, startled.

"Don't depend on that. If you insult me, I will."

"I was only repeating what my father told me."

"Your father chose to tell you a lie," said Oliver contemptuously.

"Didn't you lose your place? Tell me that."

"I did lose my place, or rather left it of my own accord."

"Wasn't there a reason for it?" insisted Roland triumphantly.

"There was a charge trumped up against me," said Oliver—"a false charge. Probably your father and your cousin were at the bottom of it. But that isn't what I care to talk about. Is there anything new in Brentville?"

"Carrie Dudley is very well," said Roland significantly.

"I am glad to hear it."

"I called there last evening. I had a splendid time," said Roland.

If Roland expected to excite Oliver's jealousy, he was not likely to succeed. Our hero knew too well Carrie Dudley's real opinion of his step-brother to feel the least fear on the subject.

"I should like to see Frank and Carrie," said Oliver quietly. "They are the only persons I regret in Brentville."

"No love lost between us," returned Roland at once, applying the remark to himself.

"Probably not," said Oliver, with a smile.

"Have you got another place?" enquired Roland curiously.

"Not yet."

"I suppose you will find it hard, as you can't bring any recommendation."

"I wouldn't accept one from Mr. Bond," said Oliver haughtily.

"How do you get along then?"

"Pretty well, thank you."

"I mean, how do you pay your expenses?" persisted Roland. "You have no income, you know."

"I ought to have," blazed out Oliver indignantly. "My mother left a hundred thousand dollars, which you and your father have coolly appropriated."

"My father has no money that is not his own," retorted Roland, "and that is more than——"

"Stop there, Roland, or I may forget myself," interrupted Oliver sternly.

There was a menace in his tone which startled Roland, and he thought it best not to complete his sentence.

"I must be going," said Roland. "Have you dined?"

He asked the question chiefly out of curiosity.

"I dined at Delmonico's," replied Oliver, in a matter-of-fact tone, enjoying Roland's amazement.

"You did!" exclaimed Roland, well aware how expensive Delmonico's famous restaurant is.

"Yes; I had a capital dinner."

"I don't believe it. You are joking," said Roland incredulously.

"What makes you say that?"

"You can't afford to dine at such a place, a boy in your position. I don't believe you have five dollars in the world."

Now was the time for Oliver to confound his incredulous enemy.

He took out the roll of bills he had recently

received and displayed it to Roland, letting him see five, ten, and twenty-dollar bills.

"I am not quite reduced to beggary, as you see," he said.

"How did you get all that money?" gasped Roland.

"I don't choose to tell you. I will only say this, that I have made more money since I left Mr. Bond's than I made while I was in his employment—three times over."

"You have?" ejaculated Roland, who was beginning to feel some respect for the boy who could make so much money, even though he disliked him. "I thought you hadn't got a place," he said, after a moment's thought.

"No more I have," replied Oliver. "I am my own employer."

"In business for yourself, hey?"

Oliver nodded.

"Well, good-morning. I'll tell Frank Dudley I have seen you."

"I wish you would."

He looked after Oliver, as he walked away, with the same feeling of wonder.

"How can a boy earn so much money?" he thought. "Oliver must be smart. I thought he'd be a beggar by this time."

In his secret heart Roland had never credited the charge of theft brought against Oliver. He didn't like him, and was ready enough to join in the charge of dishonesty fabricated by his father and Mr. Bond, but really he knew Oliver too well to believe it. Otherwise he might have suspected that Oliver's supply of money was dishonestly obtained. He concluded that his step-brother must be doing some business of a very profitable character.

With a hundred dollars in his pocket, Oliver felt justified in re-engaging the room he had in the morning resolved to leave. He managed to see John Meadows at the time of his leaving the store, and enquired if he had yet hired his old room.

"No," said John, "I am just going round there. Will you go with me?"

"It won't be necessary," said Oliver. "We had better remain where we are."

John stared.

"But how will we pay the rent?" he asked. "You have nothing."

"Haven't I? I made a hundred dollars to-day."

John whistled.

"Come, now, you're gassin'," he said.

"Does that look like gassing?" said Oliver, displaying a roll of bills.

"Good gracious! where did you get it!"

Oliver smiled.

"I thought you would be surprised," he answered. "I'll tell you the story when we get home," he said. "Now let us go and tell our landlady we have changed our minds and will keep the room."

"I'm glad we can," said John Meadows. "I felt bad about going back to my old room, and I felt anxious about you, too."

"I think I shall get along," said Oliver hopefully.

"Perhaps there is more money to be made where you made your money to-day."

"I think not. At any rate, I don't care to earn any more the same way."

The same evening Oliver strayed into a

prominent hotel on Broadway. He was alone,
his room-mate having retired early on account
of fatigue. In the smoking-room he saw, sitting by himself, a tall, bronzed, rather roughly
dressed man, evidently not a dweller in cities,
but having all the outward marks of a fron-
tiersman. Something in Oliver attracted this
man's attention, and led him to address our
hero.

"Young man," he said, "do you live in
New York?"

"Yes, sir."

"Then, perhaps you can recommend me to
a quiet house where I can obtain a lodging.
I aint used to fine hotels; they don't suit
me."

"I can recommend the house where I am
living," said Oliver. "It is quiet and comfortable, but not stylish."

"Style aint for me," said the stranger.
"If it's where you live, I'll like it better.
I like your looks and would like to get ac-
quainted with you."

"Then," said Oliver, "I'll call here to-morrow morning and accompany you to the

house. It would be too late to-night to make a change."

"That will do," said the stranger. "I will be here at nine o'clock. If you don't see me enquire for Nicholas Bundy."

CHAPTER XXII.

OLIVER ADOPTS A NEW GUARDIAN.

MRS. HILL, Oliver's landlady, was glad to obtain another lodger. She had a vacant square room which she was willing to let for five dollars a week. Oliver reported this to Nicholas Bundy at the hotel the next morning.

"If the price is too high," he added, with an involuntary glance at the stranger's shabby appearance, "perhaps Mrs. Hill will take less."

"I am willing to pay five dollars," said Nicholas promptly. "If you recommend it I have no doubt it will suit me."

When Mr. Bundy presented himself to the landlady, she, too,—for necessity had made her sharp-sighted and experience had made her suspicious,—evidently felt the same distrust as to his pecuniary status.

"Would you mind paying weekly in advance?" she asked doubtfully.

A smile lighted up his rough features.

"No, ma'am," he said; "that'll suit me just as well."

He drew out a large pouch, which appeared to be full of gold pieces, and drew therefrom an eagle.

"That'll pay for two weeks," he said, as he placed the coin in her hand.

The display of so much gold and his willingness to pay for his room two weeks in advance at once increased the lady's respect for him.

"I shall try to make your room comfortable for you," she said. "There's a sofa I can put in, and I've got an extra rocking-chair."

The stranger smiled.

"I'm afraid you'll spoil me," he said. "I'm used to roughing it, but you may put 'em in. When my young friend here comes to see me, he can sit on either."

A shabby-looking trunk and a heavy wooden box were deposited in the room before sunset.

"Now I'm at home," said Nicholas Bundy,

with satisfaction. "You'll come and see me often, won't you, Oliver?"

He had already begun to call our hero by his Christian name, and evidently felt quite an interest in him.

"I can promise that," said Oliver, "for I am a gentleman of leisure just now."

"How is that?" asked Bundy quickly.

"I have lost my situation, and have all my time at my own disposal."

"How do you pay your way, then?" enquired Nicholas.

"I have money enough on hand to last me about ten weeks, or, with rigid economy, even longer. Before that time passes, I hope to get another situation."

"How much does it cost you to live?"

"About ten dollars a week."

"Suppose I employ you for about a week," proposed Bundy.

"Is it any work I am fit for?" asked Oliver. "If so, I say yes, and thank you."

"It is something you can do. You must know that it is twenty years since I have set foot in New York, and it's grown beyond my

12

knowledge. I want to go about and see for myself what changes have taken place in it. Will you go with me?"

"Yes, Mr. Bundy, I will go with you, and charge nothing for it."

"That won't do," said the stranger. "I shall insist on paying you ten dollars a week."

"But it seems like robbing you."

"Don't you trouble yourself about that. You think I am poor, perhaps?"

"You don't look as if you were rich," said Oliver, hesitating.

"No, I suppose not," said Mr. Bundy slowly. "I don't look it, but I am worth fifty thousand dollars—in fact, more."

Oliver looked surprised.

"You wonder that I am so rough-looking— that I don't wear fine clothes, and sport a gold watch and chain. It aint in my way, boy. I've been used to roughing it so long that it wouldn't come nat'ral for me to change— that's all."

"I am glad you are so well off, Mr. Bundy," said Oliver heartily.

"Thank you, boy. It's well off in a way, I suppose, but it takes more than money to make a man well off."

"I suppose it does," assented Oliver, but he privately thought that a man with so much money was "well off" after all.

"Suppose, after twenty years' absence, you came back to your old home and found not a friend left,—that you were alone in the world, and had no one to take the least interest in you,—is that being well off?"

"That is very nearly my own situation," said Oliver. "I have a step-father, but he has cast me off."

"Did you care for him?"

"He never gave me cause to."

"Then you don't miss him?"

"He has all my mother's property,—property that should be mine,—and he cast me off with twenty dollars."

"He must be a mean skunk," said Mr. Bundy indignantly. "Tell me more about it."

Upon this Oliver told his story. Mr. Bundy listened with sympathizing interest. At one point he smote the table with his hard fist and exclaimed :

"The rhinoceros ! I'd like to hammer him with my fist ! "

"I should pity him if you did, Mr. Bundy," said Oliver smiling.

When the story was ended Nicholas took the boy's hand in his, while his rough features worked with friendly emotion.

" You've been treated bad, Oliver," he said, "but don't mind it, boy. Nicholas Bundy 'll be your friend. He won't see you want. You shan't suffer as long as I have an ounce of gold."

"Thank you, Mr. Bundy," said Oliver gratefully. "I may need your help, but, remember, I have no claim on you."

"You have as much claim as anyone. Look upon me as your guardian, and don't be anxious about the future. I, too, have been wrongly used, and some day I'll tell you the story."

Two days later, as they sat on the deck of a Staten Island steamer, Nicholas Bundy told Oliver his story.

"Twenty years ago," he said, "I was a clerk in a store in New York. I was a spruce young man then—you wouldn't think it, but I was. I was earning a moderate salary, and spending it nearly all as I went along. About this time I fell in love with a young girl of sweet face and lovely disposition, and she returned my love. I've been battered about since, and the years have used me hard, but I wasn't so then. Well, I had a fellow-clerk, by name Jones,—Rupert Jones,—who took a fancy to the same girl. But he found she liked me better, and would say nothing to him, and he plotted my ruin. He was an artful, scheming villain, but I didn't know it then. I thought him to be my friend. That made it the easier for him to succeed in his fiendish plot. I needn't dwell upon details, but there was a sum of money missing by our employers, and through this man's ingenuity it was made to appear that I took it. It was charged upon me, and my denial was disbelieved. My employers were merciful men, and they wouldn't have me arrested. But I was dismissed in disgrace, and I learned too late that he did it. I charged him with it, and he laughed in my face. 'Addie won't marry you now!' he said. Then I knew his motive. I am glad to say he made nothing by it. I resigned all claim to my betrothed, but though she consented to this, she spurned him.

"Well, my career in New York was ended. I had a little money, and, after selling my watch, I secured a cheap passage to California. I made my way direct to the mines, and at once began work. I had varying luck. At times I prospered ; at times I suffered privation. I made my home away from the coast in the interior. At last, after twenty years, I found myself rich. Then I became restless. I turned my money into gold and sailed for New York. Here I am, and I have just one purpose in view—to find my old enemy and to punish him if I get the chance."

"I can't blame you," said Oliver. "He spoiled your life."

"Yes, he robbed me of my dearest hopes. I have suffered for his sin, for I have no doubt he took the money himself."

"Do you know where he is now?"

"No; he may be in this city, If he is, I will find him.. This is the great object of my life, and you must help me in it."

"I?"

"Yes. I will take care of you. You shall not want for anything. In return, you can be my companion, my assistant, and my friend. Is it a bargain?"

"Yes," said Oliver impulsively.

"So be it, then. If you ever get tired of your engagement I will release you from it; but I don't think you will."

"Do you know, or have you any idea, where this man is—this Rupert Jones?"

"I have heard that such a man is living on Staten Island. I saw his name in the New York Directory. That is why I wished to come here to-day."

"We are at the first landing," said Oliver. "Shall we land?"

"Yes."

The two passed over the gang-plank upon the pier, and the boat went on its way to the second landing.

CHAPTER XXIII.

MR. BUNDY IS DISAPPOINTED, AND OLIVER MEETS SOME FRIENDS.

THE village lay farther up on the hill. Oliver and his companion followed the road, looking about them enquiringly.

"Suppose you find this man, what will you do ?" asked Oliver curiously.

He had an idea that Nicholas Bundy might pull out a revolver and lay his old enemy dead at his feet. This, in a law-abiding community, might entail uncomfortable consequences, and he might be deprived of his new friend almost as soon as the friendship had begun.

"I will punish him," said Nicholas, his brow contracting into a frown.

"You won't shoot him ?"

"No. I shall bide my time, and consider how best to ruin him. If he is rich, I will strip him of his wealth ; if he is respected and

honored, I will bring a stain upon his name.
I will do for him what he has done for me."

The provincialisms which at times disfigured
his speech were dropped as he spoke of his
enemy, and his face grew hard and his expression unrelenting.

"How he must hate this man!" thought
Oliver.

They stepped into a grocery store on the
way, and here Mr. Bundy enquired for Rupert
Jones.

"Do you know any such man?" he asked.

"Oh, yes; he trades here."

Nicholas Bundy's face lighted up with joy.

"Is he a friend of yours?"

"No," he replied hastily. "But I want to
see him; that is, if he is the man I mean.
Will you describe him?"

The grocer paused, and then said:

"Well, he is about thirty-five years old,
and——"

"Only thirty-five?" repeated Nicholas in
deep disappointment.

"I don't think he can be any more. He
has a young wife."

"Is he tall or short?"

"Quite tall."

"Then it is not the man I mean," said Bundy. "Oliver, come."

As they left the store he said:

"I thought it was too good news to be true. I must search for him longer; but I have nothing else to do. There are many Joneses in the world."

"Yes, but Rupert Jones is not a common name," said Oliver.

"You say right, boy, Rupert is not a common name. That is what encourages me. Well, shall we go back?"

"I think as we are over here we may as well stay a while," said Oliver. "The day is pleasant and we can look upon it as an excursion."

"Just as you say, Oliver. There is no more to be done to-day. Have you never been here before?"

"No."

"I used to come over when I was a clerk. I often engaged a boat at the Battery and rowed down here myself."

"That must have been pleasant."

"If you like rowing we can go back to the ferry pier and engage a boat for an hour."

"I should like that very much."

"I shall like it also. It is long since I did anything at rowing."

They engaged a stout row-boat, and rowed out half a mile from shore. Oliver knew something about rowing, as there was a pond in his native village, where he had obtained some practice, generally with Frank Dudley. What was his surprise when bending over the oar to hear his name called. Looking up, he recognized Frank and Carrie Dudley and their father.

"Why, it's Oliver!" exclaimed Frank joyfully. "Where have you come from, Oliver?"

"From the shore."

"I mean, how do you happen to be here?"

"Only an excursion, Frank. What brings you here? And Carrie, too. I hope are well, Carrie."

"All the better for meeting you, Oliver," said Carrie, smiling and blushing. "I have been missing you very much."

Oliver was pleased to hear this. What boy would not be pleased to hear such a confession from the lips of a pretty girl?

"I thought Roland would make up for my absence," he said slyly. "He told me when we met the other day what pleasant calls he had at your house."

"The pleasure is all on his side, then," said Carrie, tossing her head. "I hate the sight of him."

"Poor Roland! He is to be pitied!"

"You needn't pity him, Oliver," said Frank. "He loses no opportunity of trying to set us against you. But he hasn't succeeded yet."

"And he won't!" chimed in Carrie, with emphasis.

This conversation scarcely occupied a minute, though it may seem longer. Meanwhile Dr. Dudley and Nicholas Bundy were left out of the conversation. Oliver remembered this, and introduced them.

"Dr. Dudley," he said, "permit me to introduce my friend, Mr. Bundy."

"I am glad to make the acquaintance of

any friend of yours, Oliver. We are just going in. Won't you and Mr. Bundy join us at dinner in the hotel?"

Nicholas Bundy did not in general take kindly to new friends, but he saw that Oliver wished the invitation to be accepted, and he assented with a good grace. The boat was turned, and they were soon on land again.

"Who is this man, Oliver?" asked Frank in a low tone.

"He is a new acquaintance, but he has been very kind to me, and I have needed friends."

"Is it true that your step-father has cast you off? Roland has been spreading that report."

"It is true enough."

"What an outrage!" exclaimed Frank indignantly. "But, at least, he makes you an allowance out of your mother's property?"

"He sent me twenty dollars, and let me understand that I was to expect no more of him."

"What an old rascal!"

"I hate him!" said Carrie. "I would like to pull his hair."

"That's a regular girl's wish," said Frank, laughing. "Perhaps you can make it do by pulling Roland's, sis."

"I will, when he next says anything against Oliver."

"Look here, Oliver," said Frank, lowering his voice, "if you are in want of money, I've got five dollars at home that I can let you have as well as not. I'll send it in a letter."

"I've got three dollars, Oliver," said Carrie eagerly. "You'll take that, too, won't you?"

Oliver was moved by these offers.

"You are true friends, both of you," he said; "but I have been lucky, and I shall not need to accept your kindness just yet. I have nearly a hundred dollars in my pocket-book, and Mr. Bundy is paying me ten dollars a week for going around with him. But, though I don't need it, I thank you all the same."

"He looks rough," said Carrie, stealing a look at the tall, slouching figure walking beside her father; "but if he is kind, I shall like him."

"He has done more than I have yet told you. He has promised to provide for me as long as I will stay with him."

"He's a good man," said Carrie impulsively. "I'm going to thank him."

She went up to Nicholas Bundy and took his rough hand in hers.

"Mr. Bundy," she said, "Oliver tells me you have been very kind to him. I want to thank you for it."

"My little lady," said Nicholas, surprised and pleased, "if I'd been kind, that would pay me; but I've only been kind to myself. I'm alone in the world. I've got no wife nor child, nor a single relation, but I've got enough to keep two on, and as long as Oliver will stay with me he shall want for nothing. He's company to me, and that's what I need."

"I wish you were his step-father instead of Mr. Kenyon."

"What sort of a man is Mr. Kenyon?" asked Nicholas of Dr. Dudley.

"He is a very unprincipled schemer, in my opinion," was the reply. "He has managed to defraud Oliver of his mother's property and cast him penniless on the world."

"He is a scoundrel, no doubt; but I am not

sorry for what he has done," replied Mr. Bundy. "But for him I should be a solitary man. Now I have a young friend to keep me company. Let the boy's inheritance go? I will provide for him!"

They dined together, and then Dr. Dudley and his family were obliged to return.

"Shall I give your love to Roland?" asked Frank.

"I think you had better keep it yourself, Frank," and Oliver pressed his hand warmly. "You needn't tell Roland that I am prospering, nor his father, either. I prefer, at present, that they should not know it."

They parted, with mutual promises to write at regular intervals.

CHAPTER XXIV.

ANOTHER CLUE.

NICHOLAS BUNDY was disappointed by his first failure, but by no means discouraged.

"There are many Joneses in the world," he said, "but Rupert is an uncommon name. I didn't think there'd be more than one with that handle to his name. If he's alive I'll find him."

"Why don't you enquire of somebody that knew him?" asked Oliver.

"The thing is to find such a one," said Bundy. "There's been many changes in twenty years."

"Don't you know of some tradesman that he used to patronize, Mr. Bundy?"

"The very thing!" exclaimed the miner, for so I shall sometimes designate Mr. Bundy. "There's one man that may tell me about him."

"Who is that?"

"He kept a drinking-place down near Fulton Ferry. He may be living yet. I'll go and see him."

So one morning Nicholas Bundy, accompanied by Oliver, took the Third Avenue cars and went downtown. They got out near the Astor House, and made their way to the old place, which Bundy remembered well. To his great joy he found it—a little shabbier, a little dirtier, but in other respects the same.

They entered. Behind the bar stood a man of nearly sixty, whose bloated figure and dull red face indicated that he appreciated what he sold to others.

"What will you have, gentlemen?" he asked briskly.

Nicholas Bundy surveyed his countenance attentively.

"Are you Jacob Spratt?" he asked.

"Yes," answered the bartender. "Do you know me?"

"I knew you twenty years ago," answered the miner.

"I don't remember you."

"You once knew me well."

"I have seen many faces in my time. I can't remember so many years back."

"Do you recall the name of Nicholas Bundy?"

"Ay, that I do. You used to come here with a man named Jones."

"Yes—Rupert Jones. Can you tell me where he is now?"

Jacob shook his head.

"He left New York not long after you did," he answered. "He went to Chicago."

"Are you sure of that?"

"Yes, and I'll tell you why. He came here one evening and says: 'Jacob, I'm going away. You won't see me for a long time— I'm going to Chicago.'"

"Did he tell you why he was going there?"

"He said he was going there as an agent for a New York house—that he had a good chance."

"You have never seen him since?"

"No," said Jacob. Then he added meditatively: "Once I thought I saw him. There was a man I met in the street looking as like him as two peas, makin' allowance for the years he was older. I went up to him and called him by name, but he colored up and looked annoyed, and told me I was quite mistaken ; that his name wasn't Jones, but something else—I don't remember what now. Of course I axed his pardon and walked on, but he was the very picture of Rupert Jones."

"Then you feel sure that he went to Chicago ?"

"Yes, he told me so, and that was the last time I saw him. If he had stayed in the city he would have kept on comin' to my place, or I should have met him somewhere."

Nicholas Bundy thanked the old man for his information, and ordered glasses of lemonade for himself and Oliver.

"Won't you have something stronger, Mr. Bundy ?" asked the barkeeper insinuatingly.

Bundy shook his head.

"I've given up liquor," he said. "I'm better off without it, and so will the boy be. What do you say, Oliver ?"

"I agree with you, sir," said Oliver promptly.

"Lucky for me all don't think so," said Spratt. "It 'ould ruin my business."

When they left the bar-room Nicholas Bundy turned to his young companion.

"Oliver," he said, "will you go with me to Chicago?"

"I shall be glad to go," said Oliver promptly.

"Then we will start in two or three days, as soon as I have made some business arrangements."

"Mr. Bundy," said Oliver honestly, "it will cost you considerable to pay my expenses. I should like very much to go, but do you think it will pay you to take me?"

"You're considerate, boy, but don't trouble yourself about that. You are company to me, and I'm willing to pay your expenses for that, let alone the help you may give me."

"Thank you, Mr. Bundy. Then I will say no more. What day do you think you will start?"

"To-day is Tuesday. We will start on Saturday. Can you be ready?"

Oliver laughed.

"There won't be much getting ready for me," he said. "All my business arrangements can be made in half an hour."

Bundy smiled. Our hero's good spirits seemed to enliven his own. He was not only getting used to Oliver's company, but sincerely attached to him.

CHAPTER XXV.

MAKING ARRANGEMENTS.

NICHOLAS BUNDY went downtown the next morning. Contrary to his usual custom, he did not invite Oliver to accompany him.

"Perhaps you have some places to visit," he said. "If so, take the day to yourself. I shall not need you."

He proceeded to the office of a well-known broker in the vicinity of Wall Street, and, entering, looked around him. His rusty appearance did not promise a profitable customer, and he had to wait some time before any attention was paid him. Finally a young clerk came to him and enquired carelessly:

"Can we do anything for you this morning?"

"Are you one of the proprietors?" asked Nicholas.

" No," answered the young man, smiling.

" I should like to see your employer, then."

" I can attend to any little commission you may have," said the young man pertly.

" Who told you my commission was a little one, young man?"

" It seems large to him, I suppose," thought the clerk, again smiling. " If it's only a few hundred dollars——" he commenced.

" I want to consult your employer about the investment of fifty thousand dollars in gold," said Nicholas deliberately.

" Oh, I beg your pardon, sir," said the young man, his manner entirely altered. " I will speak to Mr. Hamlin at once."

Though the broker was engaged with another person he waited upon Nicholas without delay, inviting him to take a seat in his private office.

" Are you desirous of obtaining large interest, Mr. Bundy?" he asked.

" No, sir; I want something solid, that won't fly away. I've worked for my money and don't want to lose it."

" Precisely. Then I can recommend you

nothing better than Government bonds. They pay a fair interest and the security is unquestionable."

" Government bonds will suit me," said the miner. " You may buy them."

The purchase was made and Nicholas enquired :

" What shall I do with them ? I don't want to carry them around with me. Is there any place of safety where I can leave them while I am absent on a journey ? "

" Yes, sir ; you want to place them with a safe deposit company. I will give you a note to one that I can recommend."

This advice seemed good to Mr. Bundy. He presented himself at the office of the company and deposited the bonds, receiving a suitable certificate."

" One thing more," he said to himself, "and my arrangements will be made."

He visited the office of a lawyer and dictated his will. It was very brief, scarcely ten lines in length. This also he deposited with the safe deposit company.

" Oliver," he said, in the evening, " I've got

through my business sooner than I expected. Can you start to-morrow?"

"Yes, sir."

"Then we'll go. We'll pay our landlady to the end of the month, so that she can't complain. One thing more, Oliver, I want to tell you. I've left the bulk of my property, in bonds, and my will with the Safe Deposit Company, No. —— Broadway. If anything happens to me you are to go there and call for the will. Whatever there is in it I want you to see carried out."

"All right, sir."

The next day they started for Chicago.

CHAPTER XXVI.

WHO RUPERT JONES WAS.

JUST before leaving New York Oliver wrote a letter to Frank Dudley, announcing the plan he had in view.

> My new guardian, Mr. Bundy, goes to Chicago on business [he wrote] and I am to go with him. I don't know how long we shall be away. I shall be well provided for, and expect to have a good time. I may write you from the West. Remember me to Carrie, and believe me to be your affectionate friend,
>
> OLIVER CONRAD.

"So Oliver is going to Chicago," said Frank Dudley to Roland Kenyon, on the afternoon of the same day.

Roland looked surprised.

"How do you know?" he asked.

Frank showed him the passage quoted above.

"He doesn't send his love to you," said Frank mischievously.

"I don't care for his love," returned Roland, tossing his head. "I'm glad he is going to a distance."

"Why?"

"So he needn't disgrace the family."

"Are you really afraid of that?" asked Frank, in rather a sarcastic tone.

"Yes; he's a bad fellow, and you'll find it out sooner or later."

"I don't agree with you; I think Oliver a fine, manly fellow."

"Oh, I know you have always stuck up for him!" said Roland, annoyed. "You are deceived—that is all."

"Carrie is deceived, too, then," said Frank, knowing that this would tease Roland. "She has just as high an opinion of Oliver as I have."

"She'll find him out sometime," said Roland, and walked moodily away.

Reaching home, he told his father the news.

"Oliver gone to Chicago!" repeated Mr. Kenyon, with evident pleasure. "I am glad of it. I hope he'll never come back to annoy us."

"I hope so, too."

"But I am afraid he will get out of money and write for help."

"He's found some flat who has taken a fancy to him, and is paying his expenses. Very likely he'll get tired of him, though."

"Who is it?" asked Mr. Kenyon, with some curiosity.

"It's a rough sort of a man. Frank Dudley met him one day at Staten Island. An old miner from California, I believe, named Bundy."

"What!" exclaimed his father hastily and in visible agitation. "What is the man's name?"

"Bundy."

"What is his first name?"

"Nicholas, I believe."

"Is it possible?" exclaimed Mr. Kenyon, moved in some unaccountable manner. "How strange the boy should have fallen in with him!"

"Why, do you know him, father?" asked Roland, whose turn it was now to be surprised.

"I have heard of him," answered Mr. Kenyon, in an embarrassed voice; "not lately.—years ago."

"What sort of a man is he?" asked Roland, who was endowed with a full share of curiosity.

"His character was bad," answered his father briefly. "He was discharged from his place for dishonesty. I knew very little of him."

"Then he's good company for Oliver," said Roland, shrugging his shoulders. "They are well matched. I'll tell Frank Dudley what sort of a guardian his dear friend has chosen."

"I desire you will do nothing of the kind," said his father hastily.

"Why not?" asked Roland, in surprise.

"I don't care to have it known that I ever heard of the man. Frank Dudley might write to Oliver what I have said, and then it would get to the ears of this man Bundy. I have nothing against him, remember. In fact I am grateful to him for taking the boy off my hands. If we are wise, we shall say nothing to separate them."

"I see," said Roland. "I guess you're

right, father. I'd like to tell Frank, but I won't."

.   .   .   .   .

"How strange things turn out in this world!" said Kenyon to himself, when Roland had left him. "Of all men in the world Oliver has drifted into the care of the man who hates me most. It is fortunate that I have changed my name. He will never suspect that the step-father of the boy he is befriending is the man he once knew as—Rupert Jones."

CHAPTER XXVII.

A STARTLING TELEGRAM.

MEANWHILE, in her Southern prison-house, Mrs. Kenyon languished in hopeless captivity. There was only one thing to add to her unhappiness, and that was supplied by the cruel ingenuity of her unprincipled husband.

Tell her [wrote Mr. Kenyon to Dr. Fox] that her son Oliver is dead. He has just died of typhoid fever, after a week's illness. We did all we could to save him, but the disease obtained too great headway to be resisted, and he finally succumbed to it.

"If she's not insane already that may make her so," he said to himself cunningly. "I shall not tell even Dr. Fox that the story is false. If he believes it he will be the more likely to persuade her of it."

Dr. Fox did believe it. Had it been an invention he supposed Mr. Kenyon would have taken him into his confidence. So he made haste to impart the news to his patient. Essentially a coarse-minded man, he was not withheld, as many would have been, by a feeling of pity or consideration, but imparted it abruptly.

"I've got bad news for you, Mrs. Kenyon," he said, entering the room where she was confined.

"What is it?" she asked quickly.

"Your son Oliver is dead!"

She uttered one cry of deep suffering, then fixed her eyes upon the doctor's face.

"You say this to torment me," she said. "It is not true."

"On my honor, it is true," he answered; and he believed what he said.

"When did you learn it? Tell me all you know, in Heaven's name! Would you drive me mad?"

Dr. Fox shrugged his shoulders.

"I only got the letter this morning," he said. "It was from Mr. Kenyon."

"May I see the letter?"

Reflecting that it contained nothing of a private nature, Dr. Fox consented, and put

14

the letter into her hands. It carried conviction to the grief-stricken woman.

"I have nothing to live for now," she said mournfully. "My poor Oliver! So young to die!"

"Who's dead?" enquired Cleopatra, advancing to where they stood.

"My boy Oliver."

"Is that all? I thought it might be Mark Antony. Dr. Fox, have you received a letter from Antony lately?"

"No, your Majesty. If I had I would immediately have informed you."

The effect of this news was, for a time, to plunge Mrs. Kenyon into a fit of despondency. Freedom no longer had for her the old attractions. What was life to her now that her boy was dead?

Mr. Kenyon heard with pleasure of the effect produced by his cruel message.

"Why don't she die, or grow mad?" he said to himself. "I shall never feel safe while she is still alive. What would the world say if it should discover that my wife is not dead, but confined in a mad-house?"

Still, he felt moderately secure. All his plans thus far had succeeded. He had won the hand of a wealthy widow, he had put her out of the way ; he had cast off her son, appropriated her property, and there seemed to lie before him years of luxury and self-indulgence.

In the midst of this pleasant day-dream there came a rude awakening.

One day, as he was sitting in dressing-gown and slippers, complacently scanning a schedule of bonds and bank shares, a servant entered.

"Please, sir ; here's a telegram. Will you sign the book? The boy is waiting."

He took the book and signed it calmly. He was expecting a telegram from his broker, and this was doubtless the message looked for.

He tore open the envelope and read:

Your wife has escaped. We have no clue yet to her whereabouts. Fox.

He turned actually livid.

"What's the matter, sir?" asked the servant, alarmed by his appearance. "Is it bad news?"

He had his wits about him, and realized the

importance of assigning a reason for his
emotion.

"Yes, Betty, I have lost five thousand
dollars!"

"Shure the master must care a sight about
his money!" thought Betty. "He looked
just like a ghost."

Mr. Kenyon sent a message to Dr. Fox, ex-
horting him to spare no pains to capture the
fugitive. Not content with this, he followed
the telegram, taking the next train southward.

CHAPTER XXVIII.

OLD NANCY'S HUT.

MRS. KENYON'S depression and apparent submission to her fate had relaxed the vigilance of her keepers. Still, it is doubtful if she would have escaped but for the help of her insane room-mate.

Late one evening Cleopatra, with a cunning expression, showed her a key.

"Do you know what this is?" she asked.

"It is a key."

"It is the key of this door."

"How did you get it?"

Upon this point the queen would give no information. But she lowered her voice and whispered:

"Mark Antony is waiting for me outside. He is going to carry me away."

It was useless to question her delusion, and Mrs. Kenyon contented herself with asking:

"Do you mean to leave this house?"

"Yes," said Cleopatra. "Antony expects me. Will you go with me? I will make you one of my maids of honor."

"Do you think we can get out?" asked Mrs. Kenyon dubiously. "The outer door is locked."

"I know where to find the key. Time presses. Will you go?"

Believing in the death of her son, Mrs. Kenyon had supposed herself indifferent to liberty, but now that the hope of escape was was presented a wild desire to throw off the shackles of confinement came to her. What her future life might be she did not care to ask; but once to breathe the free air, a free woman, excited and exhilarated her.

"Yes; I will go," she said quickly. "Come!"

The two women dressed themselves hurriedly, softly they opened the door of their room, went downstairs, and from under the mat in the unlighted hall Cleopatra stooped down and drew out the key of the outer door.

"See!" she said exultantly.

"Quick! Open the door!" exclaimed Mrs. Kenyon nervously.

The key turned in the lock with a grating sound which she feared might lead to discovery, but fortunately it did not. A moment and they stood on the outside of their prison-house.

Now Mrs. Kenyon assumed the lead.

"Come," she said.

"Do you know where to find Mark Antony?" asked Cleopatra.

"Yes; follow me."

They did not venture to take the highway. The chances of discovery were too great. Neither knew much about the country, but Mrs. Kenyon remembered that a colored woman, sometimes employed at the asylum, lived in a lonely hut a mile back from the road. This woman—old Nancy—she had specially employed by permission of Dr. Fox, and to her hut she resolved to go.

Cleopatra, no longer self-reliant, followed her confidingly. Just on the verge of a wood, with no other dwelling near at hand, dwelt the old black woman. It was a rude cabin, dark and unpainted. Cleopatra looked doubtfully at it.

"Where are you going?" she asked, standing still. "Antony is not here."

It was not a time to reason, nor was the assumed queen a person to reason with. There was no choice but to be positive and peremptory.

"No," she answered, "Antony is not here, but here he will meet you. It is a poor place, but his enemies lie in wait for him, and he wishes to see you in secret."

This explanation suited Cleopatra's humor.

She nodded her head in a satisfied way and said:

"I know it. Augustus would murder my Antony if he could."

"Then you must not expose him to danger. Come with me."

Mrs. Kenyon advanced, not without some misgivings, since Nancy was unaware of her visit. She could hear the old woman snoring, and was compelled to knock loudly. At last old Nancy heard, and awoke in a great fright.

"Who's there?" she called out, in a quavering voice.

"It's I, Nancy. It's Mrs. Kenyon."

This only seemed to alarm the old woman the more. She was superstitious, like most of her race, and straightway fancied that it was some evil spirit who had assumed Mrs. Kenyon's voice.

"Go away, you debbil!" she answered, in tremulous accents. "I know you. You's an evil sperrit. Go away, and leave old Nancy alone."

Had her situation been less critical, Mrs. Kenyon would have been amused at the old woman's alarm, but in the dead of night, a fugitive from the confinement of a mad-house, she was in no mood for amusement.

"Don't be frightened, Nancy," she said. "I have escaped from the asylum with Cleopatra, and we want you to hide us for to-night. I will give you ten dollars if you will open your door and help us."

Now, avarice was a besetting weakness in old Nancy's character, and though Mrs. Kenyon did not know it, she had unwittingly made the right appeal to the old woman. Ten dollars was an immense sum to Nancy, who counted her savings by the smallest sums. She drew back the bolt, and opened her door, not wholly without fear that her first suspicions might be correct, and her nocturnal visitors turn out to be emissaries of Satan.

"Are you sure you aint bad sperrits?" she asked, through a narrow crevice.

"Don't be foolish, Nancy. You know me well enough, and Cleopatra, too. Open the door wider, and let us in."

Reassured in a degree by the testimony of her eyes, Nancy complied and the two entered.

"Laws, missus, it's you shure nuff," she said, "and Clopatry, too." (This was as near as she ever got to the name of the royal Egyptian.) "Who'd a thought to see you this time o' night?"

"We've run away, Nancy. You won't let Dr. Fox know?"

"I reckon not, missus. He's a drefful mean man, the old doctor is. I won't give you up to him nohow."

Luckily for Mrs. Kenyon old Nancy had

some months before had a quarrel with Dr.
Fox about some money matter in which she
felt he had cheated her. So she was glad of
this opportunity to do him an ill turn.

"Is Antony here, Nancy?" asked Cleopatra, looking about her with an air of expectation.

Nancy was about to reply in the negative,
when she caught a significant look from Mrs.
Kenyon, and altered her intended answer.

"He aint here yet, missus, but I expect
him in the morning sure."

"Likely he's her man," thought Nancy,
who was entirely unacquainted with that epi-
sode in Roman history in which Cleopatra
figured. "Likely he's her man, though she
do look old to have one."

The cabin consisted of one room on the
ground floor, but overhead was a loft covered
with straw, and used partly as a lumber-room
by the old woman. A pallet filled with straw
lay in one corner of the lower room, this being
old Nancy's bed, from which she had hastily
risen when she heard the knocking at the
outer door.

"Lie down there, honeys," she said with generous hospitality, proposing to resign her own bed to her unexpected guests.

But the position was too exposed for Mrs. Kenyon.

Looking up she espied the loft and said :

" No, Nancy, we would rather go up there. Then if Dr. Fox comes for us he won't discover us."

To this arrangement both Nancy and Cleopatra assented, and a rude ladder was brought into requisition. When they had reached the loft Cleopatra looked around her with discontent.

"Am I to lie here ?" she asked.

" Yes ; we will lie down together."

"But this is no fit couch for a great queen," she complained. "What will Mark Antony— what will my courtiers say ?"

" They will praise you for sacrificing your royal state for your lover," answered Mrs. Kenyon, who was quick-witted, and readily understood the warped mind she had to deal with.

"Then I will be content," said Cleopatra,

evidently pleased with the suggestion, "if you think Antony will approve."

"There is no doubt of it. He will love you better than ever."

Cleopatra reclined upon the straw, and was soon in a profound slumber. Mrs. Kenyon was longer awake. She was anxious and troubled, but at length she, too, yielded to sleep.

She awoke to find old Nancy bending over her.

"Don't be frightened, honey," she said; "but the old doctor is ridin' straight to the door. Don't you move or say a word, and I'll send him off as wise as he came."

Nancy had scarcely got downstairs and drawn the ladder after her, when the smart tap of a riding-whip was heard on the outer door.

Mrs. Kenyon trembled in anxious suspense.

CHAPTER XXIX.

DR. FOX IN PURSUIT.

OPENING the outer door, old Nancy counterfeited great surprise at seeing Dr. Fox mounted on horseback, waiting impatiently to have his summons answered.

"Lor' bress us!" she exclaimed, holding up both hands, "what bring you on here so airly, Massa Fox?"

"Nancy, have you seen anything of Mrs. Kenyon and Cleopatra?" asked the doctor abruptly.

"How should I see them?" asked Nancy. "I haven't been to the 'sylum sence las' week."

"They have run away," explained Dr. Fox.

"Run away! Good Lor'! What they gone and run away for?"

"Out of pure cussedness, I expect," returned the doctor in a tone of disgust. "Then you haven't seen them?—they haven't passed this way?"

"Not as I knows on. They wouldn't come to old Nancy. She couldn't help 'em."

"I was hoping you might have seen them," said Dr. Fox, disappointed. "I don't know where to look for them."

"How did they get away?" asked Nancy, fixing her round, bead-like eyes on the doctor, with an appearance of curiosity.

"I can't stop to talk," said Dr. Fox impatiently. "I must search for them, though I don't know where."

"I hope you'll find 'em, Massa Fox," said Nancy, rolling her eyes.

A sudden idea struck Dr. Fox. For a small sum he could enlist Nancy on his side, he thought.

"Look here, Nancy," he said, "these foolish woman may yet come this way. If they do, let me know in some way, so that I can catch them, and I'll give you—let me see—I'll give you five silver dollars."

"Will you really, Massa Fox?" exclaimed

Nancy, in affected delight. "Oh, golly, how rich I'll be!"

"Of course you don't get it unless you earn it, Nancy."

"Oh, I'll work for it; I will, sure, Massa Fox."

"If they come here, manage to lock them up in your cabin, and then come to me."

"You may 'pend on me, Massa Doctor. Oh, yes, you may 'pend on me."

"That secures her co-operation," thought the deluded doctor. "Five dollars is a fortune to her."

He would not have felt quite so confident if he had heard Nancy's soliloquy after his departure.

"Mean old hunks!" she exclaimed. "So he thinks he's gwine to buy old Nancy for five dollars! He's mighty mistaken, I reckon, I won't give up the poor darlings for no such money."

No doubt the ten dollars she had received from Mrs. Kenyon had its effect; but, to do old Nancy justice, she had a good heart, and, fond as she was of money, would not have sold the secret of those who put confidence in her, even if there had been no money paid her for keeping it.

Mrs. Kenyon, hidden in the loft, heard the conversation with anxiety, lest Nancy should yield to the temptation and betray her place of concealment. When the colloquy was over, and Dr. Fox had ridden away, she felt relieved.

"Thank you, Nancy," she said gratefully, peering over the edge. "You are indeed a good friend to me."

"I sent Massa Fox off with a flea in his ear," said Nancy, her portly form shaken by a broad laugh.

"I shall not forget your kindness, Nancy."

"Is Clopatry awake?" asked Nancy.

"Yes," said a smothered voice from the straw. "Is Antony come?"

"Aint seen no gemman of that name, Miss Clopatry."

"I hope he hasn't forgotten his appointment," said the queen anxiously.

"What does he look like, in case I see him, Miss Clopatry?"

15

"He looks like a prince," said Cleopatra. "He has an air of command. He's a general, you know."

"You couldn't tell me what color hair he's got!" said the practical Nancy. "I don't know much about princes."

Cleopatra looked perplexed. She had never thought particularly about the personal appearance of her hero.

"I expect it's black," she said; "but he'll ask for me. You'll know him by that."

"All right, Miss Clopatry. If I see him, I'll send him right along. Now, what 'll you have for breakfast?"

"Anything you have, Nancy. We don't want to put you to too much trouble."

"Oh, Lor', Mis' Kenyon, you needn't be afeared. What do you say, now, to some eggs and hoe-cake?"

"I would like some," said Cleopatra, brightening up. "Can I come down, Nancy?"

"Just as you please, Miss Clopatry."

"I think we may venture," said Mrs. Kenyon. "Dr. Fox will not be likely to come back at present."

The two ladies went down the ladder rather awkwardly, not being used to such a staircase. In fact, Cleopatra lost her footing, and fell in a very unqueenly attitude on the earthen floor. She was picked up, however, without having sustained any serious injury.

After breakfast Mrs. Kenyon held a consultation with Nancy as to the course she had better pursue.

"Better stay here till night, Mis' Kenyon," advised the old woman, "and then I'll take you through the woods to Scranton, where the railroad is. Ef you go now, the doctor 'll come cross you and take you back."

"Where do the cars go, Nancy? To Charleston?"

"No, Miss Kenyon. They go down souf to Georgia."

Until then Mrs. Kenyon had had no fixed plan, except it had occurred to her that it would be best to go to Charleston. But a moment's reflection satisfied her that she would be more likely to be sought after there than farther south. Dr. Fox would hardly think of following her to Georgia.

"That plan will suit me, Nancy," she said, after a short pause. "I don't much care where I go, as long as I increase the distance between me and that horrible mad-house."

"Will Clopatry go with you?" asked Nancy, indicating the queen with a jerk of her finger.

"I will ask her."

The plan was broached to Cleopatra, but it met with unexpected opposition.

"I can't go away from Antony," she said. "He is to meet me here. You said he was."

This was true, and it was found impossible to remove the impression from her mind.

Mrs. Kenyon looked at Nancy in perplexity.

"What shall we do?" she asked.

"Let her stay," said Nancy. "You can go with me. You aint goin' to be caught so easy if you are alone."

Mrs. Kenyon realized the force of this consideration. Cleopatra was really insane, and her insanity could hardly be concealed from those whom they might encounter in their flight. Dr. Fox would, of course, post notices of their escape, and Cleopatra's appearance and remarks would, in all probability, make the success of their plans very dubious.

"You are right, Nancy," said Mrs. Kenyon; "but it seems selfish to go away and leave Cleopatra here."

"The doctor didn't treat her bad, did he?" asked Nancy in a whisper.

"No."

"Then it won't do her any harm if she does get took back. It's different with you. Jest let her stay here as long as she wants to. When she finds her man don't come, she'll go back likely herself."

This was finally agreed to.

During the day there were no more visitors, much to the relief of Mrs. Kenyon.

At nightfall old Nancy and Mrs. Kenyon set out on their journey. The latter was disguised in an old gown belonging to her hostess, her gown stuffed out to like ample proportions, while a huge bonnet, also belonging to Nancy, effectually concealed her face.

"You look like my sister, Mis' Kenyon," she said. "Lor', I'd never know you!"

"I'll pass for your sister, Nancy, if any enquiry is made."

Nancy nodded acquiescence.

"That'll do," she said, in a satisfied tone. "Now, bid good-by to Miss Clopatry, and we'll go."

Cleopatra was quite willing to be left. She was quite persuaded that Antony would come for her during the evening, and urged Mrs. Kenyon to hurry him in case they met him.

For two miles Nancy and her companion travelled through the woods, until they came to the bank of a river.

"We must go 'cross here, Mis' Kenyon," she said. "There is a boat just here. Get in and I'll row you across."

Mrs. Kenyon got into the boat, and Nancy was about to put off, when a horseman rode up rapidly.

"Halt, there!" he shouted. "Who have you got with you, Nancy?"

Mrs. Kenyon's heart stood still with sickening fear, for the voice was that of Dr. Fox.

CHAPTER XXX

NANCY was not likely to turn pale, even if she had been frightened. Really, however, she was not frightened, having considerable nerve.

"Is that you, Massa Fox?" she replied composedly, pushing the boat off at the same time. "Where did you come from?"

"Who have you got with you?" demanded the doctor, in a peremptory tone.

"Lor', doctor, what's the matter? It's my sister Chloe from 'cross the river. She cum over to see me yes'day, and I'm agwine to take her home."

Dr. Fox surveyed the pretended sister critically, and was inclined to believe the story. The dress, the stuffed form, and general appearance certainly resembled Nancy. But he was not satisfied.

"Are you sure that you haven't got one of

my runaways in the boat with you?" he asked suspiciously.

Nancy's fat sides shook with laughter.

"One of them crazy critters!" she exclaimed. "Chloe, he thinks you're a crazy critter run away from his 'sylum. Won't Dinah laugh when you tell her!"

Mrs. Kenyon possessed an admirable talent for mimicry, though she had not exercised it much of late years. Now, however, the occasion seemed to call for an effort in that direction, and she did not hesitate. She burst into a laugh, rich and hearty, so like Nancy's that the latter was almost startled, as if she heard the echo of her own amusement. No one who heard it would have doubted that it was the laugh of a negro woman.

The laugh convinced Dr. Fox. He no longer entertained any doubt that it was really Nancy's sister.

"It's all right, Nancy," he said apologetically. "I see I am mistaken. If you see either of the runaways let me know," and he turned his horse from the bank.

Not a word passed between Nancy and her

passenger till they had got beyond earshot of the pursuer. Then Nancy began:

"You did dat well, Mis' Kenyon. Ef I hadn't knowed I'd have thought it was ole Chloe herself. Where did you learn dat laugh?"

"I think I might make a pretty good actress, Nancy," said Mrs. Kenyon, smiling. "I knew something must be done as Dr. Fox's suspicions were aroused. But I didn't dare to speak. I was not so sure of my voice."

"Lor', how we fooled Massa Fox!" exclaimed Nancy, bursting once more into a rollicking laugh.

"So we did," said Mrs. Kenyon, echoing the laugh as before.

"You almost frighten me, Mis' Kenyon," said Nancy. "I didn't think no one but a nigger could laugh like dat. Are you sure you aint black blood?"

"I think not, Nancy," said Mrs. Kenyon. "I don't look like it, do I?"

"No, Mis' Kenyon; you're as white as a lily; but I can't understand dat laugh nohow."

Presently they reached the other shore, and Nancy securely fastened the boat.

"How far is it to the depot, Nancy?" asked the runaway.

"Only 'bout a mile, Mis' Kenyon. Are you tired?"

"Oh, no; and if I were, I wouldn't mind, so long as I am escaping from that horrible asylum. I can't help thinking of that poor Cleopatra. I wish she might be as fortunate as I, but I am afraid she will be taken back."

"She an' you's different, Mis' Kenyon. She's crazy, an' you aint."

"Then you think I can be trusted out of the doctor's hands?"

"How came you there, anyway, Mis' Kenyon?" asked Nancy curiously.

"It is too long a story to tell, Nancy. It is enough to say that I was put there by a cruel enemy, and that since I have been confined I have met with a great loss."

"Did you lose your money, Mis' Kenyon?" asked Nancy sympathetically.

"It was worse than that, Nancy. My only boy is dead."

"Dat's awful; but brace up, Mis' Kenyon. De Lor' don't let it blow so hard on de sheep dat's lost his fleece."

"I feel that I have very little to live for, Nancy," continued Mrs. Kenyon, in a tone of depression.

"Don't you take it so much to heart, Mis' Kenyon. I've had three chil'en myself, an' I don't know where they is."

"How does that happen, Nancy?"

"When we was all slaves dey was sold away from me, down in Alabama, I reckon, and I never expec' to see any of 'em ag'in."

"That is very hard, Nancy," said Mrs. Kenyon, roused to sympathy.

"So it is, Mis' Kenyon," said Nancy, wiping her eyes; "but I hope to see 'em in a better land."

Then Nancy, pausing in her rowing, began to sing in an untrained but rich voice a rude plantation hymn:

"We'se all a-goin',
We'se all a-goin',
We'se all a-goin',
        To de Promised Land.

" We shall see our faders.
We shall see our moders,
We shall see our chil'en,
Dead an' gone before us,
In de Promised Land.

" Don't you cry, poor sinner,
Don't you cry, poor sinner,
We'se all a-goin
To de Promised Land."

"It makes me feel better to sing them words, Mis' Kenyon," said Nancy; "for it's all true. De Lord will care for us in de Promised Land."

"I am glad you have so much faith, Nancy," said her companion. "Your words cheer me, in spite of myself. For the first time, I begin to hope."

"Dat's right, Mis' Kenyon," said Nancy, heartily. "Dat's de way to talk."

They were walking while this conversation took place, and soon they reached the station —a small rude hut, or little better.

A man with a flag stood in front of it, while a gentleman and lady were standing just in the door-way.

Mrs. Kenyon had on the way disencumbered herself of the gown and other disguises which

she had worn in the boat, and appeared a
quiet, lady-like figure, who might readily be
taken for a Southern matron, with a colored
attendant.

"When will the next train start, sir?" she
asked, addressing the flagman.

"In five or ten minutes."

"Going South?"

"Yes, ma'am."

"Can I get a ticket of you?"

"The ticket agent is away. You will have
to buy one on board the train."

"Very well, sir."

They went into the small depot and waited
till the train arrived. Then Mrs. Kenyon
bade a hurried good-by to Nancy, pressed another piece of gold into her not unwilling
hand, and was quickly on her way.

As the train started she breathed a sigh of
relief.

"At last I feel that I am free!" she said to
herself. "But where am I going and what is
to be my future life?"

They were questions which she could not
answer. The future must decide.

Nancy bent her steps toward her humble home, congratulating herself on the success with which their mutual plans had been carried out.

"I wonder how Miss Clopatry is gettin' along," she reflected.

We can answer that question.

Dr. Fox, on his way back, thought he would again visit Nancy's cottage. The two refugees might possibly be in the neighborhood, although he no longer suspected Nancy's connivance with them. He was destined to be gratified and at the same time disappointed.

As he approached the house he caught sight of Cleopatra looking out of the window.

"Is that you, Antony?" she called.

Dr. Fox's face lighted up with satisfaction.

"There they are! I've got them!" he exclaimed, and quickened his horse's pace.

"Open the door, Cleopatra!" he ordered.

She meekly obeyed.

He peered round for her companion, but saw no one else.

"Where is Antony?" asked Cleopatra.

"Where is Mrs. Kenyon?" he demanded sternly.

"Gone away with Nancy," answered Cleopatra simply.

Dr. Fox swore fearfully.

"Then it was she!" he exclaimed, "after all; and I have been preciously fooled. I'd like to wring Nancy's neck!"

"Where is Antony?" asked Cleopatra anxiously.

"He is at the asylum, waiting to see you," said the doctor. "Come with me, and don't keep him waiting!"

That was enough. Poor Cleopatra put on her bonnet at once, and went back with the doctor, only to weep unavailing tears over the disappointment that awaited her.

"I'd rather it was the other one," muttered Dr. Fox. "Who would have thought she was so cunning? Where did she get that laugh? I'd swear it was a nigger!"

For three months Nancy was not allowed any work from the asylum, but she contented herself with the fifteen dollars in gold which Mrs. Kenyon had given her.

CHAPTER XXXI.

MRS. KENYON FINDS FRIENDS.

MRS. KENYON thought it best to put two hundred miles between herself and Dr. Fox. She left the cars the next morning at a town of about three thousand inhabitants, which we will call Crawford.

"Is there a hotel here?" she enquired of the depot-master.

"Yes, ma'am."

"Is it far off?"

"About three-quarters of a mile up in the village."

"Can I get a carriage to convey me there?"

"Certainly, ma'am," answered the depot-master briskly. My son drives the depot carriage. There it is, near the platform.

"Peter!" he called. "Here's a lady to go to the hotel. Have you a check for your trunk, ma'am?"

Mrs. Kenyon was rather embarrassed. She had no luggage except a small bundle which she carried in her hand, and this, she feared, might look suspicious. She had a trunk of clothing at the asylum, but of course it was out of the question to send for this.

"My luggage has been delayed," she said; "it will be sent me."

"Very well, ma'am."

Mrs. Kenyon got into the carriage and was soon landed at the hotel. It might be called rather a boarding-house than a hotel, as it could hardly accommodate more than a dozen guests. It was by no means stylish, but looked tolerably comfortable. In Mrs. Kenyon's state of mind she was not likely to care much for luxury, and she said to herself wearily:

"This will do as well as any other place."

She enquired the terms of board, and found them very reasonable. This was a relief, for she had but two hundred dollars with her, and a part of this must be expended for the replenishing of her wardrobe. This she attended to at once, and, though she studied

16

economy, it consumed about one-half of her scanty supply.

Four weeks passed. Mrs. Kenyon found time hanging heavily upon her hands. She appeared to have no object left in life. Her boy was dead, or at least she supposed so. She had a husband, but he had proved himself her bitterest foe. She had abstained from making acquaintances, because acquaintances are apt to be curious, and she did not wish to talk of the past.

There was one exception, however. One afternoon when out walking, a pretty little girl, perhaps four years of age, ran up to her, crying :

"Take me to mamma. I'm so frightened!"

She was always fond of children, and her heart opened to the little girl.

"What is the matter, my dear?" she asked soothingly.

"I've lost my mamma," sobbed the little girl.

"How did it happen, my child?"

"I went out with nurse, and I can't find her."

By enquiry Mrs. Kenyon ascertained that

the little girl had run after some flowers, while the careless nurse, not observing her absence, had gone on, and so lost her.

"What is your name, my little dear?" she asked.

"Florette."

"And what is your mamma's name?"

"Her name is mamma," answered the child, rather surprised. "Don't you know my mamma?"

Then it occurred to Mrs. Kenyon that the child was the daughter of a Mrs. Graham, a Northern visitor, who was spending some weeks with a family of relatives in the village. She had seen the little girl before, and even recalled the house where her mother was staying.

"Don't cry, Florette," she said. "I know where mamma lives. We will go and find mamma."

The little girl put her hand confidingly in that of her new friend, and they walked together, chatting pleasantly, till suddenly Florette, espying the house, clapped her tiny hands, and exclaimed joyfully:

244 ADRIFT IN THE CITY.

"There's our house. There's where mamma lives."

Mrs. Graham met them at the door. Not having heard of the little girl's loss, she was surprised to see her returning in the care of a stranger.

"Mrs. Graham," said Mrs. Kenyon, "I am glad to be the means of restoring your little girl to you."

"But where is Susan—where is the nurse?" asked Mrs. Graham, bewildered.

"I lost her," said little Florette.

"I found the little girl crying," continued Mrs. Kenyon, "and fortunately learned where you were staying. She was very anxious to find her mamma."

"I am very much indebted to you," said Mrs. Graham warmly. "Let me know who has been so kind to my little girl."

"My name is Conrad, and I am boarding at the hotel," answered Mrs. Kenyon.

She had resumed the name of her first husband, not being willing to acknowledge the tie that bound her to a man that she had reason to detest.

Mrs. Graham pressed her so strongly to enter the house that she at length yielded. In truth she was longing for human sympathy and companionship. Always fond of children, the little girl attracted her, and for her sake she wished to make acquaintance with the mother.

This was the beginning of friendship between them. Afterward Mrs. Kenyon, or Conrad, as we may now call her, called, and, assuming the nurse's place, took Florette to walk. She exerted herself to amuse the child, and was repaid by her attachment.

"I wish you'd come and be my nurse," she said one day.

"I hope you will excuse Florette," said Mrs. Graham apologetically. "She is attached to you, and is too young to know of social distinctions."

"I am very much pleased to think that she cares for me," said Mrs. Conrad, looking the pleasure she felt. "Do you really like me, then, Florette?"

The answer was a caress, which was very grateful to the lonely woman.

"It does me good," she said to Mrs. Graham. "I am quite alone in the world, and treasure more than you can imagine your little girl's affection."

"I am sure she has suffered," thought Mrs. Graham, who was of a kindly, sympathetic nature. "How unhappy I should be if I, too, were alone in the world!"

Mr. Graham was a merchant in Chicago, where business detained him and prevented his joining his wife. She was only to stay a few weeks, and the time had nearly expired when little Florette was taken sick with a contagious disease. The mercenary nurse fled. Mrs. Graham's relations, also concerned for their safety, left the sorrow-stricken mother alone in the house, going to a neighboring town to remain till the danger was over. Human nature was unlovely in some of its phases, as Mrs. Graham was to find out.

But she was not without a friend in the hour of her need.

Mrs. Conrad presented herself, and said:

"I have heard of Florette's sickness, and I have come to help you."

"But do you know the danger?" asked the poor mother. "Do you know that her disease is contagious, and that you run the risk of taking it?"

"I know all, but life is not very precious to me. I love your little daughter, and I am willing to risk my life for her."

Mrs. Graham made no further opposition. In truth, she was glad and encouraged to find a friend who was willing to help her—more especially one whom the little girl loved nearly as much as herself.

So these two faithful women watched by day and by night at the bedside of little Florette, relieving each other when nature's demand for rest became imperative, and the result was that Florette was saved. The crisis was safely past, and neither contracted the disease.

When Florette was well enough, Mrs. Graham prepared to set out for her Northern home.

"How lonely I shall feel without you," exclaimed Mrs. Conrad, with a sigh.

"Then come with us," said Mrs. Graham.

"Florette loves you, and after what has passed I look upon you as a sister. I have a pleasant home in Chicago, and wish you to share it."

"But I am a stranger to you, Mrs. Graham. How do you know that I am worthy?"

"The woman who has nursed my child back from death is worthy of all honor in my household."

"But your husband?"

"He knows of you through me, and we both invite you."

Mrs. Conrad made no further opposition. She had found friends. Now she had something to live for.

By a strange coincidence, she and Oliver reached Chicago the same day.

CHAPTER XXXII.

MR. DENTON OF CHICAGO.

IN due time, Nicholas Bundy and Oliver arrived at Chicago. They took up their residence at a small hotel, and Mr. Bundy prepared to search for some trace of Rupert Jones. He couldn't find the name in the directory, but after diligent search ascertained that such a man had been in business in Chicago ten years before. Where he went or what became of him could not immediately be learned. Time was required, and it became necessary to prolong their stay in the city.

Mr. Bundy did not care to make acquaintances. With Oliver he was not lonely. But one evening, while sitting in the public room, a stranger entered into conversation with him.

"My dear sir," he said to Mr. Bundy, "I perceive that you smoke. Won't you oblige me by accepting one of my cigars? I flatter myself that you will find it superior to the one you are smoking."

If there was one thing that Nicholas Bundy enjoyed it was a good cigar.

"Thank you, sir," he said. "You are very obliging."

"Oh, don't mention it," said the other. "The fact is I am rather an enthusiast on the subject of cigars. I would like your opinion of this one."

Nicholas took the proffered cigar and lighted it. He was sufficient of a judge to see that it was really superior, and his manner became almost genial toward the stranger who had procured him this pleasure.

"It is capital," he said. "Where can I get more like it?"

"Oh, I'll undertake that," said the other. "How many would you like?"

"A hundred to begin with."

"You shall have them. By the way, do you remain long in the city?"

"I can't tell. It depends upon my business."

"Why do you stay at a hotel? You would find a boarding-house more comfortable and cheaper."

"Do you know of a good one?"

"I can recommend the one where I am myself living. There is a chamber next to my own that is vacant, if you would like to look at it."

The proposal struck Nicholas favorably and he agreed to accompany his new acquaintance the next morning to look at it.

The house was one of fair appearance, with a tolerably good location. The chamber referred to by Denton (this was the stranger's name) was superior to the room in the hotel, while the terms were more reasonable.

"What do you say, Oliver?" asked Mr. Bundy. "Shall we remove here?"

"Just as you like, sir. It seems a very pleasant room."

The landlady was seen, and the arrangement was made for an immediate removal. She was a woman of middle age, bland in her manners, but there was something shifty and evasive in her eyes not calculated to inspire confidence. Neither Nicholas nor Oliver thought much of this at the time, though it occurred to them afterward.

"You'll find her a good landlady," said Denton, who seemed pleased at the success of the negotiations. "I have been here over a year, and I have never had anything to complain of. The table is excellent."

"I am not likely to find fault with it," said Nicholas. "I've roughed it a good deal in my time, and I aint much used to luxury. If I get a comfortable bed, and good plain victuals, it's enough for me."

"So you've been a rolling stone, Mr. Bundy," said the stranger enquiringly.

"Yes, I have wandered about the world more or less."

"They say 'a rolling stone gathers no moss,' " continued Mr. Denton. "I hope you have gathered enough to retire upon."

"I have got enough to see me through," said Nicholas quietly.

"So have I," said Denton. "Queer coincidence, isn't it? When I was fifteen years old I hadn't a cent, and being without shoes I had to go barefoot. Now I've got enough to see me through. Do you see that ring?" displaying at the same time a ring with an immense colorless stone. "It's worth a cool thousand,—genuine diamond, in fact,—and I am able to wear it. Whenever I get hard up— though there's no fear of that—I have that to fall back upon."

Nicholas examined the ring briefly.

"I never took a fancy to such things," he said quietly. "I'd as soon have a piece of glass, as far as looks go."

"You're right," said Denton. "But I have a weakness for diamonds. They are a good investment, too. This ring is worth two hundred dollars more than I gave for it."

"Is it?" asked Nicholas. "Well, all have their tastes. I'd rather have what the ring cost in gold or Government bonds."

Denton laughed.

"I see you are a plain man with plain tastes," he said. "Well, it takes all sorts of men to make a world, and I don't mind confessing that I like show."

The same day they moved into the boarding-house. It was arranged that Oliver, as before, should occupy the same room with his new gnardian, and for his use a small extra bed was put in.

"We are next-door neighbors," said Denton. "I hope you won't find me an unpleasant neighbor. The fact is, I sleep like a top all night. Never know anything from the minute I lie down till it's time to get up. Are you gentlemen good sleepers?"

"I sleep well," said Nicholas. "It's with me very much as it is with you."

"Of course you sleep well, my young friend," said the new acquaintance to Oliver. "Boys of your age ought not to wake up during the night."

"I believe I am a pretty good sleeper," said Oliver. "Why is he so particular about enquiring whether we sleep well?" thought our hero.

He was not particularly inclined to suspicion, but somehow he had never liked Mr. Denton. The man's manner was hearty and cordial, but there was a sly, searching, crafty look which Oliver had occasionally detected,

which set him to thinking. Not so with
Nicholas. He had seen much of men's
treachery, he had suffered much from it also,
but at heart he was disposed to judge favorably of his fellow-men, except where he had
special reason to know that they were
unreliable.

"Our neighbor seems very obliging," he
said to Oliver, after Denton had left the room.

"Yes, sir," answered Oliver. "I wonder
why I don't like him."

"Don't like him!" repeated Nicholas in
surprise.

"No. I can't seem to trust him."

"He appears pleasant enough," said Mr.
Bundy. "A little vain, perhaps, or he
wouldn't wear a thousand dollars on his finger. There wouldn't be many diamonds sold
if all were like me."

"I wonder what his business is?"

"He has never told me. From what he
says he probably lives upon his means."

Oliver did not continue the conversation.
Very likely his distrust was undeserved by
the man who inspired it, and he did not feel

justified in trying to prejudice Mr. Bundy against him.

Finding Nicholas was tired in the evening, Oliver went out after supper by himself. He was naturally drawn to the more brilliantly lighted streets, which, even at ten o'clock in the evening, were gay with foot passengers. Sauntering along, he found himself walking behind two gentlemen, and could not avoid hearing their conversation.

"Do you see that man in front of us?" asked one.

"The one with the diamond ring?" for the stone sparkled in the light.

"Yes; he is the one I mean."

"What of him?"

"He is one of the most notorious gamblers and confidence men in Chicago."

"Indeed! What is his name?"

"He has several—Denton, Forbes, Cranmer, and half a dozen others."

Naturally Oliver's curiosity was excited by what he heard. Passing the speakers, he scanned the man of whom they had been conversing.

It was Denton—the man who had been so friendly to Nicholas Bundy and himself.

"I was right in distrusting him," he thought. "He is a dangerous man. Now, what shall I do?"

Oliver decided not to tell Mr. Bundy immediately of what he had heard; but, for his own part, he decided to watch carefully, lest Denton might attempt in any way to injure them.

CHAPTER XXXIII.

A MIDNIGHT ATTACK.

OLIVER and his guardian retired about ten o'clock. Mr. Bundy was not long in going to sleep. Unlike Oliver, he had no care or anxiety on his mind. As we have said, he was not a man to harbor suspicion.

With our hero it was different. He knew the real character of Denton, and could not help fancying that he must have some personal object in bringing them to this house, and installing them in a room adjoining his own.

Oliver carefully locked the door, leaving the key in the lock. There was but one door, and this led into the hall.

"Now," thought our hero, "Denton can't get in except through the keyhole."

This ought to have quieted him for the night, but it did not. An indefinable suspicion, which he could not explain, made him uneasy. It was this, probably, that prompted him to go to the closet in which he knew that Nicholas Bundy kept a pistol. At times he placed the pistol under his pillow, but he had not done so to-night, considering it quite unnecessary in a quiet boarding-house.

"I don't suppose there's any need of it," thought Oliver; "but I'll take it and put it under my own pillow."

Nicholas Bundy was already asleep. He was a sound sleeper and did not observe what Oliver was doing, otherwise he would have asked an explanation.

This might have been hard to give, except the chance knowledge he had gained of Denton's character.

An hour passed and still Oliver remained awake. At about this time he heard a noise in the adjoining room as of someone moving about.

"It is Denton come home," he said to himself.

Presently the noise ceased, and Oliver concluded that his disreputable neighbor had gone to bed.

He began to be rather ashamed of his suspicions.

"Of course he can't get in here, since there is but one door, and that locked," he reflected. "It is foolish for me to lie awake all night. I may as well imitate Mr. Bundy's example and go to sleep."

Oliver was himself fatigued, having been about the streets all day, and now that his anxiety was relieved he, too, soon fell into a slumber. But his sleep was neither deep nor refreshing; it was troubled by dreams, or rather by one dream, in which Denton figured.

It was this, perhaps, that broke the bonds of sleep. At any rate, he found himself almost in an instant broad awake, with his eyes resting on a figure, clearly seen in the moonlight, standing beside Nicholas Bundy's bed examining the pockets of his coat and pantaloons, which rested on a chair close beside.

Immediately all his senses were on the alert. In one swift glance he saw all. The figure was that of Denton, and an opening in the panel between the two rooms showed how he had got in. It was clear that this was a decoy house, especially intended to admit of such nefarious deeds.

Denton's back was turned to Oliver, and he was quite unaware, therefore, that the boy had awakened. Bundy lay before him in profound sleep, and from a careless glance he had concluded that the boy also was asleep.

"Now," thought Oliver, "what shall I do? Shall I shoot at once?"

This course was repugnant to him. He had a horror of shedding blood unless it were absolutely necessary, but at the same time he was bold and resolute, and by no means willing to lie quietly and see his guardian robbed.

It was certainly a critical moment, and required some courage to face and defy a midnight robber, who might himself be armed. But Oliver was plucky, and didn't shrink.

In a clear, distinct voice he asked:

"What are you doing there?"

Denton wheeled round and saw Oliver sitting up in bed. He had a black mask over his eyes, and thought he was not recognized.

"Confusion!" Oliver heard him mutter, under his breath. "Cover up your head, boy, and don't interfere with me, or I'll murder you!" he said in a low, stern voice.

"I want to know what you are doing?" demanded our hero, undaunted.

"None of your business. Do as I tell you!" answered Denton, in a menacing tone.

"It is my business," said Oliver firmly. "You have no business here, Mr. Denton. Go back into your own room."

Denton started, and was visibly annoyed to find that he was recognized after all.

"Denton is not my name," he said. "You mistake me for somebody else."

"Denton is the name by which we know you," said Oliver. "Whether it is your real name or not I don't know or care. I know you have no business here, and you must leave instantly."

Denton laughed, a low, mocking laugh.

"You crow well, my young bantam," he said; "but you're a fool, or you would know that I am not a man to be trifled with. Cover up your head, and in five minutes you may uncover it again, and I will do you no harm."

"No, but you'll rob Mr. Bundy, and I don't intend you shall do it."

"You don't!" exclaimed the ruffian, in a tone of suppressed passion. "Come, I must teach you a lesson!"

He sprang toward Oliver's bed, with the evident intention of doing him an injury, but our hero was prompt and prepared for the attack which he anticipated. He seized the pistol and presented it full at the approaching burglar, and said coolly:

"Don't be in a hurry, Mr. Denton. This pistol is loaded, and if you touch me I will shoot."

Denton stopped short, with a feeling bordering on dismay. It was a resistance he had not anticipated. Indeed, he was so far from expecting any interference with his designs that he had come unprovided with any weapon himself.

"The boy's fooling me!" it occurred to

him. "I don't believe the pistol is loaded. I'll
find out. You must be a fool to think I am
afraid of an empty pistol," he said, looking
searchingly at the boy's face.

"You will find out whether it is loaded or
not," said Oliver coolly; "but I wouldn't
advise you to try. Just go through the same
door you came in at, and I won't shoot."

If it had been a man, Denton would have
seen that there was no further chance for him
to carry out his design; but it angered him to
give in to a boy. He felt that it was disgraceful to a man, whose strength could outmatch
Oliver twice over. Besides, he had felt
Bundy's pocket-book, and he hated to leave
the room without it.

"I'll bribe the boy," he thought. "Look
here, boy," said he; "put down that weapon
of yours. I want to speak to you."

"Go ahead!" said Oliver.

"You haven't laid down your pistol."

"And I don't intend to," said Oliver firmly.
"I am not in the habit of entertaining company in my chamber at midnight, and I prefer
to be on my guard."

Denton was enraged at the boy's coolness, but he dissembled the feeling.

"Oh, well," he said carelessly, "do as you please. Now, I've got a proposal to make to you."

"Go ahead."

"I'm very hard up, and I want money."

"So I supposed."

"The man you're with has plenty of it."

"How do you know?"

"Confound you, why do you interrupt me? You know it as well as I. Now, I want some of that money."

"That is what you came in for."

"Yes, that is what I came in for. Now, I'll tell you what I will do. I will take the money out of the pocketbook, and give you half, if you won't interfere. You can tell the old man that a burglar took the whole, and he'll believe you fast enough. So you see you will profit by it as well as I."

"You don't know me, Mr. Denton," said Oliver. "I am not a thief, and if I were I wouldn't rob the man that has been kind to me. I've heard all I want to, and you have stayed in this room long enough. If you don't disappear through that panel before I count three, I'll shoot you."

With a muttered execration, Denton obeyed, and once more Oliver found himself alone. He got up and looked at his watch. It indicated a quarter to one. What should he do? The night was less than half-spent, and Denton might attempt another entrance.

"There is no help for it," thought Oliver. "I must remain awake the rest of the night."

CHAPTER XXXIV.

DENTON SEES HIS INTENDED VICTIMS ESCAPE.

OLIVER was rejoiced to see the sunshine entering the window. He felt that his long vigil was over, and the danger was passed. He saw Bundy's eyes open, and he spoke to him.

"Are you awake, Mr. Bundy ?"

"Yes, Oliver; I have slept well, though this is a new place."

" I have not slept since midnight," said our hero.

"Why not ? Are you sick ?" asked Bundy anxiously.

"No, I was afraid to sleep."

Then, in a few words, Oliver sketched the events of the night, and added what he had heard about Denton's character.

"The skunk !" exclaimed Bundy indignantly. "But why didn't you wake me up, Oliver?"

"I would, if there had been any need of it. I was able to manage him alone."

"You're a brave boy, Oliver," said Bundy admiringly. "Not many boys would have shown your pluck."

"I don't know about that, Mr. Bundy," said Oliver modestly. "You must remember that I had a pistol in my hand and had no need to be afraid."

"It needed a brave heart and steady hand for all that. But now you must get some sleep. I am awake and there is no danger. If that skunk tries to get in he'll get a warm reception."

Oliver was glad to feel at liberty to sleep. He closed his eyes and did not open them again till nine o'clock. When he opened his eyes he saw Bundy, already dressed, sitting in a chair beside the window.

"Hallo! it's late," he exclaimed; "isn't it, Mr. Bundy?"

"Nine o'clock."

"Haven't you had your breakfast?"

"No; I am waiting for you."

"Why didn't you wake me up before? I don't like to keep you waiting."

"My boy," said Bundy in an affectionate tone, "it is the least I can do when you lay awake for me all night. I shall not soon forget your friendly devotion."

"You mustn't flatter me, Mr. Bundy," said Oliver. "You may make me vain."

"I'll take the risk."

"Have you been out?"

"Yes; I went out to get a paper, and I have seen our landlady. I gave her warning—told her I should leave to-day."

"What did she say?"

"She seemed surprised and wanted to know my reasons. I told her that I wasn't used to midnight interruptions. She colored, but did not ask any explanation. I paid her, and we will move to-day back to our old quarters. Now, when you are dressed, we will go and get some breakfast."

"Suppose we meet Denton?"

"He will keep out of our way. If he don't, I may take him by the collar and shake him out of his boots."

"I guess you could do it, Mr. Bundy," said Oliver, surveying the wiry, muscular form of his companion.

"I should not be afraid to try," said Nicholas, with a grim smile.

After breakfast they arranged to remove their trunks back to their old quarters.

"Our stay here has been short, but it has been long enough," said Nicholas. "Next time we will put less confidence in fair words and a smooth tongue."

They did not meet Denton, but that gentleman was quite aware of their movements. From the window of his chamber he saw Oliver and his guardian depart, and later he saw their luggage carried away.

"So they've given me the slip, have they?" he soliloquized. "Well, that doesn't end it. The old man is worth plucking, and the boy I am paid to watch. Confound the young bantam! I will see that he don't crow so loud the next time we meet. But why does Kenyon take such an interest in him? That's what I don't understand."

Denton took from his pocket a letter signed

"Benjamin Kenyon," and read carefully the following passage :

When you find the boy—and I think you cannot fail with the full description of himself and his companion which I send you—watch his movements. Note especially whether he appears to have any communication with a woman who may claim to be his mother. Probably they will not meet, but it is possible that they may. If so, it is important that I should be apprised at once, I will send you further instructions hereafter.

Denton folded the letter, and gave himself up to reflection.

"Why don't he take me into his confidence? Why don't he tell me just what he wants, just what this woman and this boy are to him? I suppose I have made a mistake in showing my hand so soon, and incorporating a little scheme of my own with my principal's. But I was so very hard up I couldn't resist the temptation of trying to obtain a forced loan from the old man. If that cursed boy hadn't been awake I should have succeeded, and could then have given my attention to Kenyon's instructions. I wonder, by the way, why he calls himself Kenyon. When I knew him he was Rupert Jones, and he didn't particularly honor the name, either. Well, time will make things clearer. Now I must keep my clue, and ascertain where my frightened birds are flitting to."

He went downstairs just as the expressman was leaving the house, and carelessly enquired where he was carrying the luggage. Suspecting no harm, the expressman answered his question, and Denton thanked him with a smile.

" So far, so good," he thought. " That will save me some trouble."

.   .   .   .   .

The explanation of Mr. Kenyon's letter is briefly this. His visit South had done no good. He had had an interview with Dr. Fox, in which he had so severely censured the doctor that the latter finally became angry and defiant, and intimated that if pushed to extremity he would turn against Kenyon, and make public the conspiracy in which he had joined, together with Kenyon's motive in imprisoning his wife.

This threat had the effect of cooling Mr. Kenyon's excitement, and a reconciliation was patched up.

An attempt was made to trace Mrs. Kenyon through old Nancy, but the faithful old colored woman was proof alike against threats, entreaties, and bribes, and steadily refused to give any information as to the plans of the refugee. Indeed, she would have found it difficult to give any information of value, having heard nothing of Mrs. Kenyon since they parted at the railroad station.

Nancy would have been as much surprised as anyone to hear of the subsequent escape of her guest to Chicago.

Mr. Kenyon's greatest fear was lest Oliver and his mother should meet. He knew the boy's resolute bravery, and feared the effects of his just resentment when he learned the facts of his mother's ill-treatment at the hands of his step-father. These considerations led to his opening communication with Denton, whom he had known years before, when he was Rupert Jones.

CHAPTER XXXV.

ON THE TRACK.

ONE day Nicholas Bundy entered the apartment occupied jointly by himself and Oliver, his face wearing an expression of satisfaction.

Oliver looked up from the book he was engaged in reading.

"I've found a clue, Oliver," he exclaimed.

"A clue to what, Mr. Bundy?"

"To Rupert Jones. I have ascertained that when he left Chicago he settled down at the town of Kelso, about seventy-five miles from Chicago, in Indiana."

"What do you propose to do?"

"To go there at once. Pack up your carpet-bag, and we will take the afternoon train."

"All right, Mr. Bundy."

Oliver was by no means averse to a journey.

274

He had a youthful love of adventure that delighted in new scenes and new experiences.

At two o'clock they were at the depot, and bought tickets for Kelso. They did not observe that they were watched narrowly by a red-headed man, whose eyes were concealed by a pair of green glasses. Neither did they notice that he too purchased a ticket for Kelso.

This man was Denton, who had so skilfully disguised himself with a red wig and the glasses that Oliver, though his eyes casually fell upon him, never dreamed who he was.

Denton bought a paper and seated himself just behind Oliver and his guardian, so that he might, under cover of the paper, listen to their conversation.

"What business can they have at Kelso!" he soliloquized. Then partially answering his own question, "Rupert Jones once lived there, and their visit must have some connection with him. There's something behind all this that I don't understand myself. Perhaps I shall find out. Jones was always crafty, and, as far as he could, kept his own counsel."

Denton did not glean much information from the conversation between Oliver and Bundy. The latter, though he had no suspicion of being watched, did not care to converse on private matters in a public place. He was a man of prudence and kept his tongue under control.

I have said that the three passengers bought tickets to Kelso. Kelso, however, was not on the road, and a stage for that place connected with the station at Conway. Through tickets, however, had been purchased, including stage tickets.

It was about half-past five when the cars halted at Conway. There was a small depot, and a covered wagon stood beside the platform.

Oliver, Bundy, and Denton alighted.

"Any passengers for Kelso?" asked the driver of the wagon.

"Here are two," said Oliver, pointing to Bundy.

"Anyone else?"

Denton came forward, and in a low voice intimated that he was going to Kelso.

These three proved to be the only passengers.

Now, for the first time, Oliver and his guardian looked with some curiosity at their fellow-traveller.

"He's a queer-looking customer," thought Oliver.

Bundy thought, "Perhaps he lives at Kelso, and can tell us something about it. I may obtain the information I want on the way there. I'll speak to him.

"It's a pity we couldn't go all the way by cars," he said.

"Yes," said Denton briefly.

"Do you know if our ride is a long one?"

"Six miles," answered Denton, who had enquired.

"May I ask if you live in Kelso?"

"No, sir," answered Denton.

"Perhaps you can tell me if there is a hotel there?"

"I don't know."

By this time the stranger's evident disinclination to talk had attracted Oliver's attention.

He looked inquisitively at the man with green glasses.

"There's something about that man's voice that sounds familiar," he said to himself. "Where can I have seen him before?"

Still, the red wig and the glasses put him off the scent.

Denton grew uneasy under the boy's fixed gaze.

"Does he suspect me!" he thought. "It wouldn't do for me to speak again."

When Bundy asked another question, he said :

"I hope you'll excuse me, sir, but I have a severe headache, and find it difficult to converse."

"Oh, certainly," apologized Bundy.

Denton leaned his head against the back of the carriage in support of his assertion.

The road was a bad one, jolting the vehicle without mercy. To Oliver it was fun, but Denton evidently did not relish it. At last one jolt came, nearly overturning the conveyance. It dislodged the green spectacles from Denton's nose, and for a moment his eyes were exposed. He replaced them hurriedly, but not in time. Oliver's sharp eyes detected him.

"It's Denton!" he exclaimed internally, but he controlled his surprise so far as not to say a word.

"He is on our track," thought our hero. "What can be his purpose?"

CHAPTER XXXVI.

DENTON IS CHECKMATED.

OLIVER wished to communicate his discovery to Bundy, but Denton's presence interfered. His guardian was not an observant man, and thus far suspected nothing. Before Oliver obtained any opportunity the stage reached its destination.

Kelso was a village of moderate size. A small hotel provided accommodation for passing travellers. Here the three stage passengers descended and sought accommodation. The house was almost empty, and no difficulty was experienced. Denton registered his name as Felix Graham, from Milwaukee. He registered first, and for a special reason, that the false name might divert suspicion, if any was entertained.

"Do you know our fellow-passenger, Mr. Bundy?" asked Oliver, when they were in the room assigned them, preparing for supper.

Bundy looked surprised.

"I only know that he is from Milwaukee," he answered. -

Oliver laughed.

"My eyes are sharper than yours, Mr. Bundy," he said. "He is our old acquaintance, Denton, who tried to rob you in Chicago."

Nicholas Bundy was amazed.

"How do you know?" he asked. "Surely it cannot be. Denton had black hair."

"And this man wears a red wig," said Oliver.

"Are you sure of this?" asked Nicholas thoughtfully.

"I am certain."

"When did you recognize him?"

"In the stage, when his glasses came off."

"What does this mean?" said Bundy, half to himself.

"It means that he is on our track," said Oliver coolly.

"But why? What object can he have?"

"You have asked me too much. Ask me some other conundrum."

"Can he hope to rob me again? It must be that."

"We will see that he don't."

"Possibly he has some other object in view. I should like to know."

"I'll tell you how to do it, Mr. Bundy. Will you authorize me to manage?"

"Yes, Oliver."

"Then I will take pains to mention in his presence before the landlord that we are going back to Chicago in the morning, and wish to engage seats in the stage. If he is following us he will do the same."

"A good idea, Oliver."

After supper Denton took out a cigar, and began to smoke in the office of the inn. Oliver enquired of the landlord:

"When does the stage start in the morning?"

"At eight o'clock."

"Can I engage two seats in it?"

"Yes, sir. Your stay is short."

"True, but our business takes little time to transact. Let us have breakfast in time."

Denton listened, but made no movement.

The next morning when the stage drew up before the door, not only Oliver and Bundy, but Denton also, were standing on the piazza, with their carpet-bags, ready to depart.

All got into the stage, and it set out.

It had hardly proceeded half a mile when, by previous arrangement, Bundy said suddenly :

"Oliver, I believe we must go back. There is one thing I quite forgot to attend to in Kelso."

"All right!" said Oliver. "It makes no difference to me."

The driver was signalled, and Oliver and Bundy got out.

Oliver glanced at Denton. He looked terribly amazed, and seemed undecided whether to get out also.

"Good-morning, Mr. Graham," said Oliver, with a great show of politeness. "I am sorry you will have a lonely ride."

"Good-by," muttered Denton, and the stage rolled on.

"He wanted to get out and follow us back,"

said Oliver, "but he couldn't think of any excuse."

"We have got rid of him," said Bundy; "and now I must attend to the business that brought me here."

On his return to the hotel he interviewed the landlord, and asked if he ever heard of a man named Rupert Jones.

"I should think so," answered the landlord. "He cheated me out of a hundred dollars."

"He did? How?"

"By a forged check upon the Bank of Conway. I wish I could get hold of him!" he ended.

Nicholas Bundy's eyes sparkled.

"What could you do in that case?" he enquired.

"What could I do? I could send him to State prison."

"Then you have preserved the forged check?"

"Yes, I have taken care of that."

"Mr. Ferguson," said Nicholas, "will you sell me that check for a hundred and fifty dollars?"

"Will you give it?" asked the landlord eagerly.

"I will."

"What is your object? Is this man a friend of yours?"

"No; he's my enemy. I want to get him into my power?"

"Then you shall have it for a hundred, and I hope you may catch him."

In five minutes the change was effected.

One object more Nicholas had in view. He tried to ascertain what had become of Rupert Jones, but in this he was unsuccessful. No one in Kelso had seen or heard of him for years.

CHAPTER XXXVII.

DENTON'S LITTLE ADVENTURE IN THE CARS.

WHEN Denton, to his infinite disgust, saw his scheme foiled by the return of Oliver and Bundy to the inn at Kelso, he was strongly tempted to go back also. But prudence withheld him. It was by no means certain that he had been recognized. Very probably Bundy really went back on account of some slight matter which he had forgotten.

Denton was of opinion that his visit to Kelso was not connected with the interest of his employer. Therefore he decided to return to Chicago and await the reappearance of Oliver and Bundy. Undoubtedly they would return to the same hotel where they had been stopping.

By the time he took his seat in the car he was in quite a philosophical frame of mind, and reconciled to the turn that events had taken.

It would have been well for Mr. Denton if he had become involved in no new adventures, but his lucky star was not in the ascendant.

He took a seat beside a stout, red-haired, coarse-featured man, with a mottled complexion, who might have been a butcher or a returned miner, but would hardly be taken for a "gentleman and a scholar." Yet there was something about this man that charmed and fascinated Denton. Not to keep the reader in suspense, it was an enormous diamond breast-pin which he wore conspicuously in his shirt-front. Denton knew something about diamonds, and to his practised eyes it seemed that the pin was worth at least five thousand dollars. He only ventured to glance furtively at it, lest he should excite suspicion.

The stout man proved to be sociable.

"Fine mornin'," he remarked.

"It is, indeed," said Denton, who had no objection to cultivating the acquaintance of the possessor of such a gem. "Pleasant for travelling."

"Yes, so 'tis. Speakin' of travellin', I've travelled some in my time."

"Indeed," commented Denton.

"Yes, I've just come from Californy."

"Been at the mines?"

"Well, not exactly. When I fust went out I mined a little, but it didn't pay ; so I set up a liquor saloon in the minin' deestrict, an' that paid."

"I suppose it did."

"Of course it did. You see, them fellers got dry mighty easy, and they'd pay anything for a drink. When they hadn't silver, I took gold-dust, an' that way I got paid better."

"You must have made money," said Denton, getting more and more interested.

"You bet I did. Why, they used to call me the Rich Red-head. Hallo! why, you're a red-head, too!"

Denton was about to disclaim the imputation, when he chanced to think of his red wig, and answered, with a smile:

"Queer, isn't it, that two red-heads should come together?"

"Your hair's redder than mine," said the stout man with a critical glance.

"Perhaps it is," said Denton, who was not

sensitive, since the hair belonged to a wig. "So you became rich?"

"I went to California without fifty dollars in my pocket," said the other complacently. "Now I can afford to wear this," and he pointed to the diamond.

"Dear me! why, what a splendid diamond!" exclaimed Denton, as if he saw it for the first time.

"It's a smasher, isn't it!" said the stout man proudly.

"May I ask where you got it?"

"I bought it of a poor cuss that drunk hisself to death. Gave a thousand dollars for it?"

"Why, it must be worth more!" said Denton almost involuntarily.

"Of course 'tis. It's worth three thousand easy."

"And two thousand on top of that," thought Denton. "He doesn't know the value of it. How long have you had it?" he enquired.

"Risin' six months."

"It's a beautiful thing," said Denton.

19

"Are you going to stop in Chicago, may I ask?"

"Maybe I'll stop a day, but I guess not. I live in Vermont—that is, I was raised there. I'm goin' back to astonish the natives. When I left there I was a poor man, without money or credit. Then nobody noticed me. I guess they will now," and he slapped his pockets significantly.

"Money makes the man," said Denton philosophically.

"So it does, so it does!" answered the stranger. Then, with a loud laugh at his own wit, he added: "And man makes the money, too, I guess. Ho, ho!"

Denton laughed as if he thought the joke a capital one.

"By George, I never said a better thing!" said the stout man, apparently amazed at his own wit.

"Didn't you? Then I pity you," thought Denton. But he only said:

"It's a good joke."

"So 'tis, so 'tis. Do you live in Chicago?"

"Yes; I reside there for the present."

"In business, eh?"

"No, I have retired from business. I am living on my income," answered Denton with unblushing effrontery.

"Got money, hey?" said the stout man respectfully.

"I have some," answered Denton modestly. "I am not as rich as you, of course. I can't afford to wear a breastpin worth thousands of dollars."

"Kinder gorgeous, aint it?" said the other complacently. "I like to make a show, I do. That's me. I like to have folks say, 'He's worth money.'"

"Only natural," said Denton. "What a consummate ass!" he muttered to himself.

There was a little more conversation, and then the stout man gaped and looked sleepy.

"I didn't sleep much last night," he said. "I guess I'll get a nap if I can."

"You'd better," said Denton, an eager hope rising in his breast. "A man can't do without sleep."

"Of course he can't. You jest wake me up when we get to the depot."

"Have no trouble about that," said Denton quickly. "I'll be sure to let you know."

In less than five minutes the stranger was breathing heavily, his head thrown back and his eyes closed beneath the red handkerchief that covered his face. Denton looked at him with glittering eyes.

"If I only had that diamond," he said to himself, "my fortune would be made. I'd realize on it and go to Europe till all was blown over."

Everything seemed favorable to his purpose. First, he was in disguise. He would not easily be identified as the thief by anyone who noticed his present appearance, since he would, as soon as he reached Chicago, lay aside the glasses and the wig together. Again, the man was asleep and off his guard. True, it was open day, and there were twenty other passengers in the car at the very least. But Denton had experience. He had begun life as a pickpocket, though later he saw fit to direct his attention to gambling and other arts as, on the whole, a safer and more lucrative business.

Denton riveted his eyes covetously on the captivating diamond. His fingers itched to get hold of it. Was it safe? A deep snore from the stout man seemed to answer him.

"What a fool he is to leave such a jewel in open sight!" thought Denton. "He deserves to lose it."

An adroit movement, quick as a flash, and the pin was in his possession. He timed the movement just as the cars reached a way station, and he instantly rose, with the intention of leaving the car.

But he reckoned without his host.

As he rose to his feet his companion dashed the handkerchief from his face, rose also, and clutched him by the arm.

"Not so fast, Mr. Denton," he said, in a tone different from his former one. "You've made a little mistake."

"Let go, then!" said Denton. "I am going to get out."

"No, you are not. You are going back to Chicago as my prisoner."

"Who are you?" demanded Denton, startled.

The red-headed man laughed.

"I am Pierce, the detective," he said. "We have long wanted to get hold of you, and I have succeeded at last, thanks to the diamond pin. By the way, the diamond is false—a capital imitation, but not worth over ten dollars. You may as well give it up."

"Is this true?" asked Denton, his face showing his mortification.

"You can rely upon it."

"I'll buy it of you. I'll give you twenty dollars for it."

"Too late, my man. You must go back with me as a prisoner. Suppose we take off our wigs. My hair is no more red than yours."

He removed his wig, and now, in spite of his skin, which had been stained, Denton recognized in him a well-known detective, whose name was a terror to evil-doers.

"It's all up, I suppose," he said bitterly. "I don't mind the arrest so much as the being fooled and duped."

"It's diamond cut diamond—ha! ha!" said

the detective—"or, we'll say, red-head *versus* red-head."

When Denton reached Chicago he became a guest of the city—an honor he would have been glad to decline.

CHAPTER XXXVIII.

THE MEETING AT LINCOLN PARK.

FOR weeks Oliver and his mother had lived in the same city, yet never met. Each believed the other to be dead; each had mourned for the other. No subtle instinct led either to doubt the truth of the sad reports which, for base ends, Mr. Kenyon had caused to be circulated.

But for her unhappy domestic troubles, Mrs. Conrad (for she had assumed the name of her first husband) was happily situated. Mrs. Graham was bound to her by the devoted care which she had taken of the little Florette. Indeed, the bereaved woman had come to love the little girl almost as if she were her own, and had voluntarily assumed the constant care of her, though regarded as a guest in the house.

Mr. Graham was very wealthy, and his

house, situated on the Boulevard, was as attractive as elegance and taste, unhampered by a regard for expense, could make it. A spacious, well-appointed chamber was assigned to Mrs. Conrad, and she lived in a style superior to which she had been accustomed. Surely it was a fortunate haven into which her storm-tossed bark had drifted. If happiness could be secured by comfort or luxury, then she would have been happy. But neither comfort nor luxury can satisfy the heart, and it was the heart which, in her case, had suffered a severe wound.

One day, as Mrs. Graham and Mrs. Conrad sat together, the little Florette in the arms of the latter, Mrs. Graham said:

"I am afraid you let that child burden you, Mrs. Conrad. She never gives you a moment to yourself."

Mrs. Conrad smiled sadly.

"I don't wish to have a moment to myself. When I am alone, and with nothing to occupy me, I give myself up to sad thoughts of the happiness I once enjoyed."

"I understand," said Mrs. Graham gently,

for she was familiar with Mrs. Conrad's story. "I can understand what it must be to lose a cherished son."

"If he had only been spared to me I believe I could bear without a murmur the loss of fortune, and live contentedly in the deepest poverty."

"No doubt; but would that be necessary? Certainly your husband has no claim to the fortune, which he withholds from you."

"I suppose not."

"If you should make the effort you could doubtless get it back."

"Probably I could."

"You had better let me ask Mr. Graham to select a reliable lawyer whom you could consult with reference to it."

Mrs. Conrad shook her head.

"Let him have it," she said. "I care nothing for money. As long as you, my dear friend, are content to give me a home I am happier here than I could be with him."

"My dear Mrs. Conrad, it would indeed grieve me if anything should take you from us, even if to your own advantage. You see

how selfish I am ? But I can't bear to think
that that brutal husband of yours is enjoying
your money, and thus reaping the benefit of
his bad deeds."

"Sometimes I feel so," Mrs. Conrad admitted. "If Oliver were alive I should feel
more like asserting my rights, but now all
ambition has left me. If I should institute
proceedings I should be compelled to return
to New York, where everything would remind
me of my sad loss. No, my dear friend, your
advice is no doubt meant for the best, but I
prefer to leave Mr. Kenyon in ignorance of
my whereabouts and to keep away from his
vicinity. You don't want me to go away,
Florette, do you ?"

"Don't doe away," pleaded the little
girl, putting her arms round Mrs. Conrad's
neck.

"You little darling!" said Mrs. Conrad,
returning the embrace. "I have something
to live for while you love me."

"I love you so much," said the child.

"I don't know but what I shall become
jealous," said Mrs. Graham playfully.

"Go and tell your mamma that you love her best," said Mrs. Conrad.

She felt that a mother's claim was first, beyond all others. Nothing would have induced her to come between Florette and the affection which she owed to her mother.

Little Florette ran to her mother and climbed in her lap.

"I love you best, mamma," she said, "but I love my other mamma, too."

"And quite right, my dear child," said Mrs. Graham, with a bright smile. "It was but in jest, Mrs. Conrad. No mother who deserves her child's love need fear rivalry. Florette's heart is large enough and warm enough to love us both."

Mrs. Conrad rejoiced in the liberty to love Florette and to be loved by her, and if ever she forgot her special cause of sorrow it was when she had the little girl in her arms.

"I have a favor to ask of you, Mrs. Conrad," said Mrs. Graham, a little later.

"It is granted already."

"This afternoon I want to pay some calls. Will you be willing to go out with Florette?"

"Most certainly. I shall be glad to do so."

"I am sorry I cannot place the carriage at your disposal, as I should like to use it myself."

"Oh, we can manage without it. Can't we, Florette?"

"Let us yide in the horse-cars," said the little girl. "I like to yide in the cars better than in mamma's carriage."

"It shall be as you like, Florette," said Mrs. Conrad.

Florette clapped her little hands. Accustomed to ride in the carriage, it was a change and variety to her to ride in the more democratic conveyance, the people's carriage.

Mrs. Conrad, intent on amusing her little charge, decided to take her to Lincoln Park, in the northern division of the city. This is a beautiful pleasure-ground, comprising over two hundred acres, with fine trees, miniature lakes and streams, and is a favorite resort for children and their guardians, especially on Saturday afternoons, when there are open-air concerts. It was a bright, sunny day, and even Mrs. Conrad felt her spirits enlivened as she descended from the cars, and, entering the park, mingled with the gay throngs who were giving themselves up to enjoyment.

Little Florette wanted to go to the lake, and her companion yielded to her request.

It was early autumn. The trees had lost none of their full, rich foliage, and the lawns were covered with soft verdure. Little Florette laughed and clapped her hands with childish hilarity. Mrs. Conrad sat down on the grass, while Florette ran hither and thither as caprice dictated.

"Don't go far away, Florette," said Mrs. Conrad.

"No, I won't," said the child.

But a child's promises are soon forgotten. She ran to the lake, and while standing on the brink managed to tumble in. It was not deep, yet for a little child there was danger. Florette screamed, and Mrs. Conrad, hearing her cry, sprang to her feet in dismay.

But Florette found a helper.

Oliver had strayed out to Lincoln Park like the rest in search of enjoyment, and was standing close at hand when the little girl fell into the lake.

It was the work of an instant to plunge in and rescue the little girl. Then he looked about to find out to whom he should yield her up.

His eyes fell upon Mrs. Conrad hastening to her young charge. As yet she had not noticed Oliver. She only saw Florette.

Oliver's heart gave a great bound. Could it be his mother—his mother whom he believed dead—or was it only a wonderful resemblance?

"Mother!" he exclaimed, almost involuntarily.

At that word Mrs. Conrad turned her eyes upon him. She, too, was amazed, and something of awe crept over her as she looked upon one whom she thought a tenant of the tomb.

"Oliver!" she said wistfully, and in an instant he was folded in her arms.

"Then it is you, mother, and you are not dead!" exclaimed Oliver joyfully, kissing her.

"Did you think me dead, then? Mr. Kenyon wrote me that you were dead."

"Mr. Kenyon is a scoundrel, mother; but I can forgive him—I can forgive everybody, since you are alive."

"God is indeed good to me. I will never murmur again," ejaculated Mrs. Conrad, with heartfelt gratitude.

"But, mother, I don't understand. How came you here—in Chicago?"

"Come home with me, Oliver, and you shall hear. My little Florette's clothes are wet, and I must take her home immediately."

A cab was hired, for delay might be dangerous. On the way Mrs. Conrad and Oliver exchanged confidences. Oliver's anger was deeply stirred by the story of his mother's incarceration in a mad-house.

"I take back what I said. I won't forgive Mr. Kenyon after that!" he said. "He shall bitterly repent what he has done!"

CHAPTER XXXIX.

THE COMMON ENEMY.

MRS. GRAHAM heartily sympathized in the joy of the mother and son, who, parted by death, as each supposed, had come together so strangely.

"You look ten years younger, Mrs. Conrad," she declared. "I never saw such a transformation."

"It is joy that has done it, my dear friend. I was as one without hope or object in life. Now I have both."

"Your husband has your fortune yet."

"I care not for that. Oliver is more to me than money."

"Thank you, mother," said Oliver; "but we must be practical, too. I have learned that money is a good thing to have. Mr. Kenyon has been led to wrong us, and make us unhappy, by his greed for money. We will punish him by depriving him of it."

"I quite agree with you, Oliver," said Mr. Graham, who was present. "Your step-father should be punished in the way he will feel it the most."

"What course would you advise me to pursue, Mr. Graham?" asked Oliver.

"I am not prepared with an immediate answer. We will speak of it to-morrow."

Learning how much kindness Oliver had received from Nicholas Bundy, Mrs. Conrad invited him to bring his friend with him in the evening, and the invitation was cordially seconded by Mr. Graham.

Nicholas was overjoyed to hear of the good fortune of Oliver, but hesitated at first to accept the invitation.

"I'm a rough backwoodsman, Oliver," he said. "In my early life I was not so much a stranger to society, but now I shan't know how to behave."

"You underrate yourself, Mr. Bundy," said Oliver. "I can promise you won't feel awkward in my mother's society, and Mrs. Graham is very much like her."

Nicholas looked doubtful.

"You judge me by yourself, my boy," he answered. " Boys adapt themselves to ladies' society easy, but I'm an old crooked stick that don't lay straight with the rest of the pile."

"I don't care what you are, Mr. Bundy," said Oliver, with playful imperiousness ; "my mother wants to see you, and come you must!"

Nicholas Bundy laughed.

"Well, Oliver," he said, "things seem turned round, and you have become my guardian. Well, if it must be, it must, but I'm afraid you'll be ashamed of me."

"If I am, Mr. Bundy, set me down as a con- ceited puppy," said Oliver warmly. "Haven't you been my kind and constant friend?"

Nicholas looked pleased at Oliver's warm- hearted persistence.

"I'll go, Oliver," he said. "Come to think of it, I should like to see your mother."

When Nicholas and Oliver entered the ele- gant Graham mansion, the former looked a little uneasy, but his countenance lighted up when Mrs. Conrad, her face genial with smiles, thanked him warmly for his kindness to her boy.

"I couldn't help it, ma'am," he said. "I've got nobody to care for except him, and I hope you'll let me look after him a little still."

"I shall never wish to come between you, Mr. Bundy. I am glad that he has found in you a kind and faithful friend. His step-father, as you know, has been his worst enemy and mine. I hoped he would prove a kind and faithful guardian to my boy, but I have been bitterly disappointed."

"He's a regular scamp, as far as I can learn," said Nicholas bluntly. "You haven't got a picture of him, have you? I should like to know how the villain looks."

"I have," said Oliver. "This morning, in looking over my carpet-bag, I found an inner pocket, in which was a photograph of Mr. Kenyon. I believe Roland once used the bag, and in that way probably it got in."

"Have you the picture here?" asked Mr. Bundy.

"Here it is," answered Oliver, drawing it from his pocket.

Nicholas took it, and as he examined it his face wore a look of amazement.

"Who did you say this was?" he asked.

"Mr. Kenyon."

"Your step-father?"

"Yes."

"It is very singular," he remarked, in an undertone, his face still wearing the same look of wonder.

"What is very singular, Mr. Bundy?" Oliver asked curiously.

"I'll tell you," answered Nicholas Bundy slowly. "This picture, which you say is the picture of your step-father, is the picture of Rupert Jones, my early enemy."

Both Oliver and his mother uttered exclamations of surprise.

"Can this be true, Mr. Bundy?"

"There is no doubt about it, ma'am. It is a face I can never forget. There is the same foxy look about the eyes—the same treacherous smile. I should know that face anywhere, and I would swear to it in any court in the United States."

"But the name! My step-father's name is Kenyon."

"Names are easily changed, Oliver, my boy.

The man's real name is Rupert Jones. I don't care what he calls himself now. He's misused us all. He's been my worst enemy, as well as yours, ma'am, and yours, Oliver. Now, I move we both join forces and punish him."

"There's my hand, Mr. Bundy," said Oliver.

"He's your husband, ma'am," said Nicholas, "What do you say?"

"I was mad to marry him; I will never live with him again. I am out of patience with myself when I think that through my means I have brought misfortune upon my son."

"I don't look upon it just that way, ma'am," said Bundy. "But for that, I might never have met Oliver or you, and that would have been a great misfortune. He's played a desperate game, but we've got the trump cards in our hand, and we'll take his tricks."

"I fear that he may harm you," said Mrs. Conrad. "He is a bad man."

"That is true enough, but I think I shall prove a match for him. I've got a little document in my pocket which I think will checkmate him."

"What is that?"

"A note which he has forged. I picked it up at Kelso."

The next day a consultation was held, and it was decided that Oliver and his mother and Mr. Bundy should go on to New York at once, and that hostilities should be initiated against Mr. Kenyon.

During the day a note was received from the city prison, to this effect:

I have a secret of importance to your young friend, to divulge. Come and see me.
DENTON.

"Shall you go, Mr. Bundy?" asked Oliver!

"Certainly. It is worth while to strengthen our evidence as much as possible."

"May I go with you?"

"I wish you would. You are the most interested, and it is proper that you should be present."

There was no opposition made on the part of the authorities, and Oliver and Mr. Bundy were introduced into the presence of the prisoner.

Denton smiled.

"You see I'm hauled up for moral repairs," he said coolly. "Well, it's my luck."

"Did you have a pleasant return from Kelso, Mr. Denton?" asked Oliver.

"So you recognized me?"

"Yes, in spite of your red wig!"

"Someone else recognized me, too—a detective. That is why I am here. But let us proceed to business."

"Go on."

"I can give you information of importance touching this boy's step-father."

"Perhaps we know it already."

"It is hardly likely. His name is not Kenyon. I can tell you his real name."

"It is Rupert Jones," said Bundy.

"Where the deuce did you learn that?" asked Denton, astonished.

"I recognized his picture. Is that all you have to tell us?"

"No. I have been in his employ. As his agent, I dogged you."

"Prove that to us, and we will give you a hundred dollars."

"Make it a hundred and fifty."

"Done!"

Denton placed in the hands of Nicholas Bundy his letters of instruction from Mr. Kenyon.

"They will help our case," said Nicholas. "I think we shall be able to bring our common enemy to terms."

CHAPTER XL.

THE THUNDERBOLT FALLS.

MR. KENYON returned from the South baffled in his enquiries about his wife. Henceforth his life was one unceasing anxiety. He had pretended that his wife was dead, and she might at any time return alive to the village. This would place him in a very disagreeable position. He might, indeed, say that she was insane, and that he had been compelled to place her in an asylum. But everybody would ask: "Why did you not say this before? Why report that your wife was dead?" and he would be unprepared with an answer.

Indeed, he feared that the discovery of his conduct would make him legally liable to an unpleasant extent.

We already know that he had employed Denton to dog the steps of Oliver and Bundy. All at once Denton ceased to communicate

with him. For five days not a word had come
to him from Chicago. He naturally felt
disturbed.

"What has got into Denton? Why doesn't
he write to me? Can he have betrayed me?"

This is what he said to himself one morning as he sat at his desk in the house which
had once been his wife's.

"If I could only sell this place even at
a sacrifice, I would go to Europe, taking
Roland with me," he muttered. "Even as it
is, perhaps it will be as well."

Mr. Kenyon looked at the morning paper,
searching for the advertisement of the Cunard
Line. "A steamer sails on Saturday," he
read, "and it is now Tuesday. I will go to
the city to-morrow and engage passage. In
Europe I shall be safe. Then if my wife
turns up I need not fear her."

At this point a servant—one recently
engaged—came to the door of his room and
informed him that a gentleman wished to see
him.

"Do you know who it is?" he enquired.

"No, sir. I never saw him before."

"Bring him up, then; or, stay—is he in the parlor?"

"Yes, sir."

"I will see him there."

Mr. Kenyon came downstairs quite unprepared for the visitor who awaited him.

He started back when his glance fell on Oliver.

"Why do you come here?" he demanded with a frown.

"That is a strange question to ask, Mr. Kenyon. This is the house where I was born. It was built by my father. It ought to be mine."

"Indeed!" answered Kenyon, with a sneer.

"You know it as well as I do, sir."

"I know that the place is mine, and that you are an intruder."

"Upon what do you rest your claim, Mr. Kenyon?" asked our hero.

"Upon your mother's will, as you know very well."

"I don't believe that my mother would make a will depriving me of my rightful inheritance."

"I care very little what you believe. The will has been admitted to probate and is in force. I don't think it will do you any good to dispute it."

"Where did my mother die, Mr. Kenyon?" demanded Oliver, looking fixedly at his step-father.

"Can he have met his mother?" thought Kenyon, momentarily disturbed. But he inwardly decided in the negative. Of course they might meet some day, but then he would be in Europe and out of harm's reach.

"You know very well where she died."

"Do you object to tell me?"

"I object to answering foolish questions. What is your motive in reviving this melancholy subject?"

"I want to ask you to have my mother's remains brought to this town and laid beside the body of my father in our family tomb."

"He is still in the dark!" thought Mr. Kenyon.

"Impossible!" he answered.

"That's true enough," thought Oliver.

"Have you any other business?" asked his step-father.

"I wish you to give me a fair portion of the property which my mother left."

Mr. Kenyon smiled disagreeably. He felt his power.

"Really, your request is very modest," he answered, "but it can't be complied with."

"Mr. Kenyon, do you think it right to deprive me of all share in my father's property?"

"You have forfeited it by your miscon duct," said his step-father decisively.

Just then the door opened, and Roland entered.

"Has he come back?" he demanded dis agreeably.

"He has favored us with a call, Roland," said Mr. Kenyon. "He thought we might be glad to see him."

"I wonder he has the face to show himself in this house," said Roland.

"Why?" asked Oliver.

"Oh, you know why well enough. You are a common thief."

"Roland Kenyon, you will see the time when you will regret that insult, and that very soon," said Oliver, with honest indignation.

"Oh, shall I? I'm not afraid of you," retorted Roland.

"I permit no threats here," said Mr. Kenyon angrily.

"He is safe for the present," said Oliver.

"Thank you for nothing," said Roland. "Father, how long are you going to let him stay in the house?".

"That is not for your father to say, Roland," said Oliver coolly.

"What do you mean, you young reprobate?" demanded the step-father angrily. "If you have come here to make a disturbance, you have come to the wrong place, and selected the wrong man. Will you oblige me by leaving the house?"

Oliver sat near the window. He saw, though neither of the others did, that a carriage stood at the gate, and that Nicholas Bundy and a New York lawyer were descending from it. The time had now come for a change of tone.

"Mr. Kenyon," he said, "My answer is briefly that this house is not yours. I have a better right here than you."

"This insolence is a little too much!" exclaimed his step-father, pale with passion. "Leave this house instantly or I will have you put out!"

Before there could be an answer the bell rang. Mr. Kenyon put a restraint on himself.

"Go out at once," he said, "I have other visitors who require my attention."

The door opened, and the lawyer and Mr. Bundy were admitted. To Mr. Kenyon's surprise both nodded to Oliver. It was revealed to him that they were his friends.

"Gentlemen," he said, with less courtesy than he would otherwise have shown, "I do not know you. I am occupied, and cannot spare you any time this morning."

"We cannot excuse you, Mr. Kenyon," said Nicholas Bundy. "We come here as the friends of this boy, your step-son. My companion is Mr. Brief, a lawyer, and my name is Bundy—Nicholas Bundy."

Mr. Kenyon winced at this name.

"I don't understand you," he said. "We have no business together. I must request you to excuse me."

"Plain words are best," said the lawyer. "Mr. Kenyon, I am authorized to demand your instant relinquishment of the property and estates of the late Mr. Conrad."

"In whose favor?" asked Mr. Kenyon, whose manner betrayed agitation.

"In favor of Oliver Conrad and his mother."

"His mother is dead!" said Kenyon nervously; "and by her will the property is mine."

"The will is a forgery."

"Take care what you say, sir. I require you to prove it."

"I shall prove it by Mrs. Conrad herself."

As he spoke, Mrs. Conrad, who had been in the carriage, entered the room. She never spoke to her husband, but sat down quietly, while Roland stared at her, open-mouthed, as at one from the grave.

"Father," he exclaimed, "didn't you tell me she was dead?"

21

"She never died, but was incarcerated by your father in an insane asylum, while he forged a will bequeathing him the property," said the lawyer. "Well, Mr. Kenyon, what have you to say?"

"Gentlemen, the game is up," said Kenyon sullenly. "I played for high stakes, and have lost. That's all."

"You have placed yourself in the power of the wife you have wronged. You could be indicted for forgery and conspiracy. Do you admit that?"

"I suppose I must."

"What have you to say why we should not so proceed?"

"Spare me, and I will go away and trouble you no more."

"First, you must render an account of the property in your possession, and make an absolute surrender of it all."

"Would you leave me a beggar?" asked Kenyon, in a tone of anguish.

"If so, we should only treat you as you treated your step-son. But my client is merciful. She is willing to allow you and your son an annuity of five hundred dollars each, on condition that you leave this neighborhood and do not return to it."

"It is small, but I accept," said Mr. Kenyon sullenly.

"For your own good, I advise you to go to-day, before your treatment of your wife becomes known in the village," said Mr. Brief. "Call at my office in the city, and business arrangements can be made there."

"I am willing," said Kenyon.

"Wait a minute, Kenyon," said Nicholas Bundy, "I've got a word of advice. Don't go to Kelso, in Indiana."

"Why not?" asked Kenyon mechanically.

"Because you look so much like a certain Rupert Jones, who once flourished and forged there, that there might be trouble. I used to know Rupert Jones myself, and he did me an injury. You remember that. I have wanted to be revenged for years, but I am satisfied now. Once you were up and I was down. Now it's the other way. I am rich, and when I die, that boy"—pointing to Oliver—"is my heir."

Roland looked as if a thunderbolt had fallen. He had never been aware of his father's perfidy before. He had himself acted meanly, but at that moment Oliver pitied him.

"Roland," said he, "I once thought I should enjoy this moment, but I don't. I wish you good luck. Will you take my hand?"

Roland's thin lips compressed. He hesitated, but hate prevailed.

"No," he answered. "I won't take your hand. I hate you!"

"I am sorry for it," said Oliver. "I am glad you won't be unprovided for, and won't suffer. If ever you feel differently, come to me."

Mr. Kenyon and Roland left the house together, and took the first train for the city. They called at the office of Mr. Brief, and the final arrangements were concluded. Oliver and his mother came back to their own, and Nicholas Bundy came to live with them. Oliver concluded his preparations for college, where in due time he graduated.

Three years later Mr. Kenyon died, by a

strange coincidence, in an insane asylum. Then Roland, chastened by suffering and privation, for his father had squandered their joint allowance on drink, and many times he had fasted for twenty-four hours together, came back to his old home, and sought a reconciliation with those he had once hated. He was generously received, a mercantile position was found for him, his old allowance was doubled, and he grew to like Oliver as much as he had once detested him.

If Mrs. Conrad is ever married again it will be to Mr. Bundy, who is her devoted admirer. Oliver has decided to become a lawyer. If he carries out his purpose, he will always be ready to champion the cause of the poor and the oppressed. He is engaged to Carrie Dudley, and the wedding will take place immediately after he is admitted to the bar. The clouds are dispersed, and henceforth, we may hope, his pathway will be lighted by sunshine to

THE END.

HORATIO ALGER, JR.

———

The enormous sales of the books of Horatio Alger, Jr., show the greatness of his popularity among the boys, and prove that he is one of their most favored writers. I am told that more than half a million copies altogether have been sold, and that all the large circulating libraries in the country have several complete sets, of which only two or three volumes are ever on the shelves at one time. If this is true, what thousands and thousands of boys have read and are reading Mr. Alger's books! His peculiar style of stories, often imitated but never equaled, have taken a hold upon the young people, and, despite their similarity, are eagerly read as soon as they appear.

Mr. Alger became famous with the publication of that undying book, "Ragged Dick, or Street Life in New York." It was his first book for young people, and its success was so great that he immediately devoted himself to that kind of writing. It was a new and fertile field for a writer then, and Mr. Alger's treatment of it at once caught the fancy of the boys. "Ragged Dick" first appeared in 1868, and ever since then it has been selling steadily, until now it is estimated that about 200,000 copies of the series have been sold.

—"Pleasant Hours for Boys and Girls."

———

A writer for boys should have an abundant sympathy with them. He should be able to enter into their plans, hopes, and aspirations. He should learn to look upon life as they do. Boys object to be written down to. A boy's heart opens to the man or writer who understands him.

—From "Writing Stories for Boys," by Horatio Alger, Jr.

RAGGED DICK SERIES.

6 vols.   By Horatio Alger, Jr. $6.00

Ragged Dick.   Rough and Ready.
Fame and Fortune.   Ben the Luggage Boy.
Mark the Match Boy.   Rufus and Rose.

TATTERED TOM SERIES—First Series.

4 vols.   By Horatio Alger, Jr. $4.00

Tattered Tom.   Phil the Fiddler.
Paul the Peddler.   Slow and Sure.

TATTERED TOM SERIES—Second Series.

4 vols. $4.00

Julius.   Sam's Chance.
The Young Outlaw.   The Telegraph Boy.

CAMPAIGN SERIES.

3 vols.   By Horatio Alger, Jr. $3.00

Frank's Campaign.   Charlie Codman's Cruise.
Paul Prescott's Charge.

LUCK AND PLUCK SERIES—First Series.

4 vols.   By Horatio Alger, Jr. $4.00

Luck and Pluck.   Strong and Steady.
Sink or Swim.   Strive and Succeed.

LUCK AND PLUCK SERIES—Second Series.

4 vols. $4.00

Try and Trust.   Risen from the Ranks.
Bound to Rise.   Herbert Carter's Legacy.

BRAVE AND BOLD SERIES.

4 vols.   By Horatio Alger, Jr. $4.00

Brave and Bold.   Shifting for Himself.
Jack's Ward.   Wait and Hope.

VICTORY SERIES.

3 vols.   By Horatio Alger, Jr. $3.00

Only an Irish Boy.   Adrift in the City.
Victor Vane, or the Young Secretary.

FRANK AND FEARLESS SERIES.

3 vols.   By Horatio Alger, Jr. $3.00

Frank Hunter's Peril.   Frank and Fearless.
The Young Salesman.

GOOD FORTUNE LIBRARY.

3 vols.   By Horatio Alger, Jr. $3.00

Walter Sherwood's Probation. A Boy's Fortune.
The Young Bank Messenger.

HOW TO RISE LIBRARY.

3 vols.   By Horatio Alger, Jr. $3.00

Jed, the Poorhouse Boy.   Rupert's Ambition.
Lester's Luck.

COMPLETE CATALOG OF BEST BOOKS FOR BOYS AND GIRLS
MAILED ON APPLICATION TO THE PUBLISHERS

THE JOHN C. WINSTON CO., PHILADELPHIA

J. T. TROWBRIDGE.

NEITHER as a writer does he stand apart from the great currents of life and select some exceptional phase or odd combination of circumstances. He stands on the common level and appeals to the universal heart, and all that he suggests or achieves is on the plane and in the line of march of the great body of humanity.

The Jack Hazard series of stories, published in the late *Our Young Folks*, and continued in the first volume of *St. Nicholas*, under the title of "Fast Friends," is no doubt destined to hold a high place in this class of literature. The delight of the boys in them (and of their seniors, too) is well founded. They go to the right spot every time. Trowbridge knows the heart of a boy like a book, and the heart of a man, too, and he has laid them both open in these books in a most successful manner. Apart from the qualities that render the series so attractive to all young readers, they have great value on account of their portraitures of American country life and character. The drawing is wonderfully accurate, and as spirited as it is true. The constable, Sellick, is an original character, and as minor figures where will we find anything better than Miss Wansey, and Mr. P. Pipkin, Esq. The picture of Mr. Dink's school, too, is capital, and where else in fiction is there a better nick-name than that the boys gave to poor little Stephen Treadwell, "Step Hen," as he himself pronounced his name in an unfortunate moment when he saw it in print for the first time in his lesson in school.

On the whole, these books are very satisfactory, and afford the critical reader the rare pleasure of the works that are just adequate, that easily fulfill themselves and accomplish all they set out to do.—*Scribner's Monthly.*

JACK HAZARD SERIES.

6 vols.   By J. T. TROWBRIDGE $7.25

Jack Hazard and His Fortunes   Doing His Best.
The Young Surveyor.   A Chance for Himself.
Fast Friends.   Lawrence's Adventures.

CHARLES ASBURY STEPHENS.

"This author wrote his "Camping Out Series" at the very height of his mental and physical powers.

"We do not wonder at the popularity of these books; there is a freshness and variety about them, and an enthusiasm in the description of sport and adventure, which even the older folk can hardly fail to share."—*Worcester Spy.*

"The author of the Camping Out Series is entitled to rank as decidedly at the head of what may be called boys' literature."—*Buffalo Courier.*

CAMPING OUT SERIES.
By C. A. STEPHENS.

All books in this series are 12mo. with eight full page illustrations. Cloth, extra, 75 cents.

CAMPING OUT. As Recorded by "Kit."

"This book is bright, breezy, wholesome, instructive, and stands above the ordinary boys' books of the day by a whole head and shoulders."—*The Christian Register,* Boston.

LEFT ON LABRADOR; OR, THE CRUISE OF THE SCHOONER YACHT "CURLEW." As Recorded by "Wash."

"The perils of the voyagers, the narrow escapes, their strange expedients, and the fun and jollity when danger had passed, will make boys even unconscious of hunger."—*New Bedford Mercury.*

OFF TO THE GEYSERS; OR THE YOUNG YACHTERS IN ICELAND. As Recorded by "Wade."

"It is difficult to believe that Wade and Read and Kit and Wash were not live boys, sailing up Hudson Straits, and reigning temporarily over an Esquimaux tribe."—*The Independent,* New York.

LYNX HUNTING: From Notes by the Author of "Camping Out."

"Of *first quality* as a boys' book, and fit to take its place beside the best."—*Richmond Enquirer.*

FOX HUNTING. As Recorded by "Raed."

"The most spirited and entertaining book that has as yet appeared. It overflows with incident, and is characterized by dash and brilliancy throughout."—*Boston Gazette.*

ON THE AMAZON; OR, THE CRUISE OF THE "RAMBLER." As Recorded by "Wash."

"Gives vivid pictures of Brazilian adventure and scenery."—*Buffalo Courier.*

THE RENOWNED STANDARD JUVENILES

BY EDWARD S. ELLIS

Edward S. Ellis is regarded as the later day Cooper. His books will always be read for the accurate pen pictures of pioneer life they portray.

LIST OF TITLES

DEERFOOT SERIES
Hunters of the Ozark.
The Last War Trail.
Camp in the Mountains.

LOG CABIN SERIES
Lost Trail.
Footprints in the Forest.
Camp Fire and Wigwam.

BOY PIONEER SERIES
Ned in the Block-House.
Ned on the River.
Ned in the Woods.

THE NORTHWEST SERIES
Two Boys in Wyoming.
Cowmen and Rustlers.
A Strange Craft and Its Wonderful Voyage.

BOONE AND KENTON SERIES
Shod with Silence.
In the Days of the Pioneers.
Phantom of the River.

WAR CHIEF SERIES
Red Eagle.
Blazing Arrow.
Iron Heart, War Chief of the Iroquois.

THE NEW DEERFOOT SERIES
Deerfoot in the Forest.
Deerfoot on the Prairie.
Deerfoot in the Mountains.

TRUE GRIT SERIES
Jim and Joe.
Dorsey, the Young Inventor.
Secret of Coffin Island.

GREAT AMERICAN SERIES
Teddy and Towser; or, Early Days in California.
Up the Forked River.

COLONIAL SERIES
An American King.
The Cromwell of Virginia.
The Last Emperor of the Old Dominion.

FOREIGN ADVENTURE SERIES
Lost in the Forbidden Land.
River and Jungle.
The Hunt of the White Elephant.

PADDLE YOUR OWN CANOE SERIES
The Forest Messengers.
The Mountain Star.
Queen of the Clouds.

ARIZONA SERIES
Off the Reservation; or, Caught in an Apache Raid.
Trailing Geronimo; or, Campaigning with Crook.
The Round-Up; or, Geronimo's Last Raid.

OTHER TITLES IN PREPARATION

PRICE $1.00 PER VOLUME   Sold separately and in set

Complete Catalogue of Famous Alger Books, Celebrated Castlemon Books and Renowned Ellis Books mailed on application.

THE JOHN C. WINSTON CO.   PHILADELPHIA, PA.

www.ingramcontent.com/pod-product-compliance
Lightning Source LLC
Chambersburg PA
CBHW020934030726
47496CB00005B/1177